D1270583

Paid in Blood 2

Lock Down Publications and Ca$h
Presents

Paid in Blood 2

A Novel by *Hood Rich*

Paid in Blood 2

Lock Down Publications
P.O. Box 870494
Mesquite, Tx 75187

Visit our website @
www.lockdownpublications.com

Copyright 2019 Hood Rich
Paid in Blood 2

First Edition October 2019
Printed in the United States of America

Lock Down Publications
Like our page on Facebook: Lock Down Publications @
www.facebook.com/lockdownpublications.ldp
Cover design and layout by: **Dynasty Cover Me**
Book interior design by: **Shawn Walker**
Edited by: **Sunny Giovanni**

Stay Connected with Us!

Text **LOCKDOWN** to 22828 to stay up-to-date with new
releases, sneak peaks, contests and more...
Thank you.

Submission Guideline.

Submit the first three chapters of your completed manuscript to ldpsubmissions@gmail.com, subject line: Your book's title. The manuscript must be in a .doc file and sent as an attachment. Document should be in Times New Roman, double spaced and in size 12 font. Also, provide your synopsis and full contact information. If sending multiple submissions, they must each be in a separate email.

Have a story but no way to send it electronically? You can still submit to LDP/Ca$h Presents. Send in the first three chapters, written or typed, of your completed manuscript to:

LDP: Submissions Dept
Po Box 870494
Mesquite, Tx 75187

DO NOT send original manuscript. Must be a duplicate.

Provide your synopsis and a cover letter containing your full contact information.

Thanks for considering LDP and Ca$h Presents.

Hood Rich

Chapter 1
Binkey

Getting used to being in the county jail wasn't that hard. After a while, I simply adapted. I whooped three broads' asses over trying me because I'm small. After that, them hoes didn't mess with me no more. Majority of the females were plugged in gangs, but I had so much going on that my irritation was at an all-time high, when this one bitch became my first example. We were coming back from the gym, me rushing so that I could get to the shower before the other girls came and used up all the hot water.

The showers held ten women at a time. It was an open space with a pole that had ten shower heads on it going around in a circle. By the time I got into the shower I was number two and was showering away when I noticed I had forgotten my shampoo. I had the conditioner, just not the shampoo. It was left on the bench in front of the shower. So, I dipped out for no less than ten seconds to grab it, when I turned back to my shower head, and there was this bull dyke in my shower, laughing and mugging me like everything was kosher.

I sucked my teeth. My heart began to race because I knew I was going to have to show this bitch what was good. I walked right back into the shower where she was. "Uh, excuse me, but this is my shower. I just went to get my shampoo."

She grunted, allowing the water to beat on her face before filling her mouth with it and spitting on my toes. "You move, you lose." She bellowed, giving me an intimidating stare.

I thought this bitch was nuts. This nasty, obese, monster of a tramp had just spat that nasty ass water out her mouth and onto my foot. I know she didn't. I nodded. "Okay."

I went over to the sink and poured out half of my shampoo, filled the rest with water, and shook it up. I looked over to the bull dyke and saw she was talking away with her back turned to me. I finished with what I was doing, and naked, slipped into the shower and tapped her on her back. When she turned around, I squirted the soap deep within her eyes, turned to my side and elbowed her square in the face while she screamed, reaching out trying to grab me, but she was blinded. I hit her with another elbow straight on, then put her in a headlock and crashed the top of her head into the shower wall. By this time, the other females had cleared the shower and watched the show. After her head crashed into the wall, she passed out; her body went limp. I straddled her and pummeled her face with blow after blow. Her blood pooled down the drain with the rest of the shower water. Once I knew that she was out cold, I kicked her to the side and finished my shower. The other girls watched me with their eyes bugged. I didn't pay them any attention.

The next day, the bull dyke got sent up to Dwight Corrections. She'd been awaiting transfer. She was sentenced to 75 years in prison for killing her lover and the man she caught her cheating with. She said that she'd catch me on the rebound. I wasn't worried.

The second event happened two months after the first. I'd returned early from rec one day, only to find my cellmate pleasuring herself to Heaven's son, who was essentially my nephew. She was an older woman of about 38. I flew into the room and snatched the picture from her hand. It was Tarig Junior at one of his swim meets. I turned to her with a disgusted look on my face.

She started to explain herself immediately. "Look, sista, I'm sorry. It's been a long time. I saw naked skin. Before I knew it, I—"

I had already blacked out. I slammed our cell door, flashed back to her and kicked her straight in the face. "Sick ass bitch!"

The sista had some fight in her. Even though blood spurted everywhere, she still tackled me with a piercing scream. I fell against the bars with her arms tightly around my waist. I could hear her breathing hard, still apologizing.

"Bitch, let me go! Come on! You woman enough to finger yourself off some little kid, bitch, you should be woman enough to fight me head up, so let me go!" I was eager to get at her ass. Tarig Junior was my heart, and this bitch had the nerve to be violating his image. I wanted her ass, bad.

She still wasn't trying to let me go. When I felt her teeth biting into my thigh, that's when I lost it. I jerked my knee up with all my might and caught her square in the chin. She let me go, then I caught her with another knee, then two lefts, and a right. Then, I blanked out, left, right, left, right. Before I knew it, blood was all over my face and the guards was struggling to get our cell open. When they finally did, they yanked me out. I kicked her one more time in the face before they drug me to the isolation room, which was their form of the hole.

Hood Rich

Chapter 2
Roman

"I searched all of them ma'fuckas. Ain't none of them cats have no money on them. That was a hit from the beginning, bro; trust me."

"How did you know though? What made you beat them niggas to the punch?"

"Bro, 'cause this dope dealing shit ain't my forte; whacking ma'fuckas is. I know when the heat is on, and they was finna charge us to get to that dope. I baited that fool. Any hustler ain't gone care who else dope you got, long as you got his. When they found out we had more than his dope in the car, his eyes got big as saucers. He gave his lil' henchmen a signal that I caught and it's because of that signal that we still alive and them niggas is changed over."

Champ looked over to me and gave me that eye that said thank you and he appreciated me saving his life. "Yo, I owe you, fool."

"Never, joe. It's all a part of the game. What we need to find out is why JJ would send us on that mission if he didn't know what was really good with them niggas."

"Yo, I'm all over that. I'ma meet with Moeshe personally about this. I got a feeling that it's more to it that meets the eye."

Back in Chicago he dropped me off at Binkey's crib and told me that he would be in touch.

Binkey opened the door looking tired. She leaned forward and kissed me on the cheek, then walked off straight into the kitchen. "Boy, go take a shower. You smell like death and gun powder. I'ma heat your food up and then you can tell me what's good."

I did just that. After I got clean and told her what happened, she simply shook her head.

"But that's what I love about you. You have those great killer instincts. My only worry is when God gon' take those away from you, and essentially take you away from me. I keep having the worst of dreams every night, and whenever you aren't in my bed, holding me all night though." She crossed herself like the Catholics do, then started mumbling under her breath. I noticed that she was starting to do that a lot lately.

She put on some old Keith Sweat. He sang, *"I will never do anything to hurt you..."* I nodded at those lyrics and pulled her in close to me, wrapping my arms around her. "Ma, what matters is that I'm alive." I kissed her forehead.

She laid her head on my chest as we stood there. "I know that, baby, but for how long?" I felt her holding me tighter.

Keith Sweat sang on, but her question played over and over in my head, uninterrupted.

The next day, Mya came over, so Binkey and I took her out to Noah's Ark. Of course she had to go get her lil' friend Candance which meant I had to dodge a million and one questions as to why I hadn't gotten back to her mother. After everyone I answered, she popped a new one, until she killed me with her last statement.

"Roman, I don't know how you gon' take this, but I'm pregnant." She shoved some papers in front of me that she had gotten from her doctor. "It must have happened the first few times we were together. I wasn't gon' say nothing until I was absolutely sure, but I am, so…"

I kept re-reading the paperwork over and over in my head. I had so many thoughts going through my head I thought my brain was going to explode. The first thing I did was call Binkey into the house. I was so damn defeated. I prepared myself for the outburst that was sure to come from her as soon as she found out what I already knew. Kelly stood across the living room, looking at me as if I had lost my mind, but the only thing I was thinking about was getting all this shit over and done with right now. I couldn't believe that I had allowed myself to be so reckless. It's like they say, sometimes the penis does get the best of a nigga.

Binkey came into the house smiling. When she saw my expression, everything in her face became distorted. She put her hand over her stomach and looked worried. She looked from Kelly back to me. "Roman, what's wrong?"

I shook my head, then handed her the paperwork.

She scrunched up her face and sucked her teeth. She flipped the paper over to see if any writing was on the back, then shoved them into my chest. "And? So, what's the purpose of you handing me this?" Her tone was starting to get harsh.

Kelly tried to fade into the kitchen. I called her name and told her to chill. "Look, Roman, I don't want no drama. I was just trying to let you know what the deal was."

Just then, Mya and Candance ran into the living room laughing. "Daddy, what's taking you so long?

Can we go already? You know if we get there late we gon' have to wait in long lines for everything, then you gon' get mad and it'll ruin everybody's day." She was tugging my shirt, the sunlight reflecting off of her beautiful face.

"Baby, go wait in the car. Me and Binkey will be there in just a moment. Let us finish discussing grown folks' business." I kissed her on the forehead.

She smiled. "Come on, Candance. We gotta do what my father says or else we won't be going nowhere." She grabbed her friend's hand and they slowly walked back outside.

As soon as they left, it was like the whole aura of the room changed. Binkey quietly closed the door behind them. Then she opened the curtains so we could keep an eye on them. Once she was sure they would be okay, she walked up to me and swung, trying to slap me, but I ducked. Then she upped a machete from the small of her back and ran full speed at Kelly, who fell, then got up in a haste to get away.

Before she could catch her, I caught up to her and wrapped my arms around her from the back. She turned her neck and bit me on the shoulder. Pushing her head backward, she tried to head-butt me.

"Girl, calm yo' ass down. What the fuck is wrong with you?"

"Let me go, Roman, you cheating son-of-a-bitch! You better let me the fuck go now! You're hurting me and the baby!"

I didn't know if she was telling the truth or not, so I eased up just a lil' bit, still very conscious of the machete in her hand. "Binkey drop that big ass sword boo. Calm yo' ass down so we can talk about this shit like adults!"

"Like adults?" She wiggled with all of her might trying to break loose. When she realized that I wasn't going to let her go she began to calm down. "Alright, I'm cool, Roman, just let me go."

I stayed conscious of the machete, but by that time I was so irritated that I was ready for whatever. If she was going to try and get at me with that blade, then I'd just have to go for what I know. I definitely wasn't gon' let her slice me with that ma'fucka. I let her go.

She straightened out her dress and turned around slowly to face me, still holding the big blade. "Who is that bitch, and when did you start fucking her? Was it before or after me, Roman? Look me in the eye while you answer these questions." I had never seen her angrier than she was at that moment.

My expression was blank. You know that face you get when you know you caught, and it ain't nothing you can do about it besides keep it real and face up to your wrong doings? I felt like that. I felt like the world was crashing down on me and there was nowhere for me to run. What's crazy is that I also felt humbled and ready to get everything over and done with. I had never told Binkey that I was ready to settle down with just her or nobody else for that matter. Don't get me wrong, over the last couple weeks I had been definitely considering certifying her as my one, but in my own mind I hadn't done that as of yet.

"Boo."

"Nigga, don't boo me right now. Just tell me what's good, and remember, you looking me right in the eye."

I gazed into her brown beauties and kept shit one hunnit. "Both. I fucked with her before and after, but not since. I've gotten serious with you in my own heart."

Her expression was a look of confusion. "What you mean by that? What do you mean that you ain't messed with her since you got serious with me within your heart?" She spat nastily.

"Come on, Binkey, you know my lifestyle, shorty. You know how I get down. I ain't never considered being with just no one female until I met you. And boo, even so, it still has taken some will power within myself to be faithful to just you. This shit is a process."

Her eyes bugged out. "A process. Oh, okay, so it's hard for you to keep shit one hunnit with me? It's that hard for you to be faithful when you supposed to love me, and been loving me ever since we were kids. Why do you get to pick when to be faithful, but as soon as you see a nigga glance my way you be ready to kill his ass? So, imagine what you would do if I lay on my back and let some nigga jump up and down between my legs. And what if I told yo' ass that I was going through a process?" Tears were pouring down her cheeks at this point. "Then you got the nerve to get this girl pregnant, when I'm standing here, already pregnant with your child. I just don't get it."

Damn, I hated when a female I cared about cried. That shit broke me up, especially when I was the cause. So many excuses got to running through my head, but none of them made sense. I wanted to wrap my arms around her, but I felt that would have been a mistake. I was stuck. "Binkey, baby, listen." I knelt down in front of her. "I fucked up, boo. Huh." I tilted my head back and exposed my Adams apple. "Go ahead, Ma. Do you! Boo, I fucked up. I betrayed you, so right that shit." I swallowed, preparing for her to change me over.

She grabbed my chin with tears in her eyes and raised her arm all the way in the air with the machete in it. "I'm sorry, boo." I saw her face become distorted, then she bit into her bottom lip and was coming down with the machete at full speed.

Just then there was a beating on the door, then Kelly yelled, "Come in, officer, the door is open! Hurry up because this bitch is crazy! She finna kill him!"

The door was kicked in, and in three seconds the house was flooded with so many policemen and women that it seemed like we were in the police station. They handcuffed Binkey and snatched me up, slamming me against the wall.

"Say, man, what the fuck is your problem? Quit handling her like that! She pregnant."

"Calm down, sir, and let us do our job." A bald-headed, muscle-bound, tall police officer said as he pushed me harder into the wall.

They took Binkey out in cuffs. She was silent. Didn't utter a sound as they loaded her into the squad car. Behind me I heard Kelly telling everything that had taken place. She exaggerated the story so much that by the end, Binkey sounded like a cold-blooded killer, and was on the verge of killing me right before they intervened. Now I don't know how true the last part was, but what I did know was that I had to get my shorty out of them cuffs.

The officer holding me released me. "Are you okay, son?"

"Yo, B, don't call me son. I ain't yo' child. Y'all gotta let my baby momma go. She pregnant, and she ain't did nothing wrong."

I saw them picking up the machete and dropping it into a triple plastic evidence bag. An officer with a camera took pictures of it while his partner wrote down word for word what Kelly was telling her.

The girls finally came in. Mya was crying, and Candance was doing everything that she could to console her.

Mya came right up to me and wrapped her arms around my waist. "Daddy, they got Binkey in the police car and she crying. When I tried to talk to her the policeman screamed at me and told me to get away from his prisoner."

I wrapped my right arm around her, telling her that everything was going to be okay. That was Thursday afternoon. They didn't give Binkey a bail hearing until a week later which was unusual for Cook County. They usually gave you those the same or next day. All week I had been trying to visit Binkey, but she refused them. I sent her an attorney and she rejected him too. No matter what I tried to do to help her, she refused my every advance. So, I had to settle for seeing her at the bail hearing.

She came through the door in the courtroom with those ugly familiar oranges on. Both her hands and feet were shackled. It looked like her belly had grown since she'd been in there. Her face, even without make-up, was beautiful. Below her eyes were slight traces of sleep deprivation. She looked weary yet strong. As she was going to stand beside her attorney our eyes met and held for a few seconds. Within hers I saw compassion, then in a quick change they turned cold. She turned her back on me.

The judge rambled on and on about the purpose of the bail hearing, what she was being charged with, and asked the state to make its argument.

The District Attorney, a heavy-set lady with red hair, stood up. "Your honor, at this time we are content with hearing from the defendant's side as to appropriate bail."

The judge, a red-faced old man with an angry snarl, looked over to Binkey's attorney and nodded. "How say you?"

Her attorney stood up. A sharp dressed sista who resembled Angela Bassett. "Your honor, we request that the defendant be let go on her own recognizance. She has no priors, has lived in the city of Chicago for twenty-eight years. She is pregnant and has no means or purpose to flee. This incident was just the curse of having a bad day; it happens to the best of us. She is extremely apologetic. My client acted off of pure emotions after finding out that her child to be's father had gotten another woman pregnant." She shook her head to add dramatic effect.

"Is that all, Mrs. Ryan?"

"Yes, your honor."

The District Attorney stood back up. "Your honor, at this time we are asking that the defendant be denied bail. We have just been given serious information that involves the defendant's weapon in a double murder. According to our source, traces of DNA were found deep within the ridges of Ms.

Green's blade."

There was a whole bunch of murmuring going on. Binkey slumped in the seat behind her and passed out. The bailiff rushed over to her just as visions of blood started to appear between her legs. He screamed for a doctor on his walkie-talkie.

I was perplexed. I didn't know what to do. I was completely caught off guard. *Double murder! DNA caught between the blades!* I know baby girl was smarter than that. I was accustomed to seeing her clean that blade thoroughly. I tried to remember if I recalled her doing that after we'd changed over Moe and Tim. Damn, I couldn't. Fuck, now that I remembered, that was the night we had sexed for the first time. We threw all caution to the wind. And the next day I don't remember if she did it then or not. In fact, I think we fucked for damn near twenty-four hours straight after the first time. At least it felt like it anyway.

The paramedics ran into the courtroom and took her out. I hurried and ran out, jumping in my whip and speeding to Cook County Hospital. When I got there the nurse at the desk confirmed that Binkey came in but that I wasn't eligible to visit with her because she was under arrest. No matter how much I snapped and told her that she was having my kid prematurely, or that I needed to be there to support her, the nurse was not letting me get the information to what room she was being housed in. So finally, I gave up and ran around the whole pregnancy ward until I found an officer standing outside one of the delivery rooms.

I approached him with caution. "Say, man, that's

my baby's moms in there."

Through the door I heard Binkey screaming and the nurse yelling for her to push. She kept screaming, "It's too early! Please! My child! My God, it is way too early!"

I started to feel sick on the stomach. I got to imagining the wrong kinds of everything. I didn't know what I would do if something happened to Binkey or our child. Before I even knew I was doing it, I dropped to my knees and planted my forehead directly to the floor. Then I lifted myself by the waist but remained on my knees. I turned my palms up and started begging Allah for a safe delivery and a healthy baby boy.

I always felt odd calling on the Divine when I was in a jam, but Allah knows best, and the Koran teaches us that that is what Allah is there for; that's why He is the Beneficent and the most Merciful. I repeated over and over in my head, "In the name of Allah, the Beneficent, the most Merciful. All praises and worships are for Allah alone. The Cherisher, and Sustainer of all worlds. The Beneficent, the Most Merciful. Master of the day of judgement. You alone do we worship. Your aid do we seek. Lead us unto the straight path. The path of those upon whom You have bestowed Your grace. Whose portions are not worth, and do not go astray Ameem.... Aaahhmeemmm.

Over and over I repeated this prayer, known to the Muslim culture as the Afatih`ah, while rocking back and forth on my knees, listening to all of the commotion behind me. I must have said it a thousand times before I heard my son screaming. I jumped up and watched the nurses wrap him in a blanket, then rushed him out the room. Ten or more doctors ran into the room where Binkey was frantic. They closed the door and my heart dropped.

Chapter 3
Scooby

Even though I loved fucking with Amanda, her two kids were driving me crazy. They had to be the baddest lil' boys that I ever came in contact with. If you left them alone for one second you can guarantee that when you went back to where they were, they would have destroyed something. I tried my best to be more than fatherly to the lil' bad asses too, but that role was taking a toll on me physically. No matter what I did or what I bought their lil' asses, an hour later after they promised me or their mother that they were going to be good, they would be fucking up again.

They were five and three years old. They almost looked like twins. Both had long hair and caramel skin like their mother, brown eyes, and slim. It seemed that the older son was the follower and the three-year-old was the leader. They didn't listen to nobody, and they drove their mother crazy. She did all that she could to be the best mother to them, but no matter how hard she tried, they always found a way to make her job that much harder.

And, yeah, she whooped their ass. She would run into her room and come back with a belt and wear their lil' asses out. They would holler and scream and promise not to do whatever they had done anymore, and she would relent. An hour later they would have broken something else, or one of them would have a bloody nose from the other one punching him in it. They fought like cats and dogs all the time. Most times it was like they weren't even brothers. And she would always break them up with an ass whoopin'.

I was trying my best to dial back on my crack smoking. But after babysitting them for six hours straight while she was gone taking care of some personal business, I would have gone crazy had I not been able to take a few blasts. Sometimes I was so thankful for that white poison. I closed the bathroom door, closed the lid to the toilet and sat down. I blew two ten-dollar rocks back to back until I was lifted. *Whoo!* I felt good and energized.

The kids were in the living room. I bought them both a big ass bucket of ice cream and a small cake. They each had their own bucket and their own cake. I didn't care if they ate it all either, just as long as they shut the fuck up. I was losing my patience. It had been a while since I dealt with some kids.

When I came out of the bathroom, I peeked into the living room and they were still sitting on the floor in front of the television watching Teenage Mutant Ninja Turtles. They were so engrossed in the program that they were barely eating their dessert. There were two large hamburger and cheese pizzas on the kitchen table I had also bought, but they wanted their desserts first, and who was I to argue with how they wanted to eat their food, and in what order? The main thing was that they were eating and that they were quiet. I still couldn't believe that.

I had been messing with Amanda for six months by then. I was honestly starting to care about her even though I knew that was dangerous. Her boyfriend, baby daddy, whatever, was set to come home in less than a year. I knew that she would be going back to him, which is why I kept my emotions in check. I supported her because I understood her struggle. But beyond that the reality of our future always remained at the forefront of my brain.

Just as I was grabbing a slice of pizza I heard keys turning in the lock and in came Amanda talking on her cell phone a mile a minute. She stepped on her tippy toes and kissed me on the cheek, holding up one finger. She started to nod then said her goodbyes to whoever was on the phone.

"Hey, baby, how were the boys?" She lifted up the pizza box, raised an eyebrow, watching me bite into my slice.

I chewed, opening a can of crème soda. Took a long swallow, then nodded. "They were okay." I ain't wanna tell her that they drove me crazy. That they fought for an hour straight after she left. Or that I had to bribe them with buying all the stuff for them to behave. So, I simply nodded, knowing that I would never be the one to get caught babysitting again.

I think she knew that I was holding something back because she gave me a sympathetic look and stroked my cheek. "Aww, poor baby. It wasn't that bad was it?" She wrapped her arms around my neck and kissed me on the lips. "It's okay, daddy, I'ma make it up to you later on. You know I got you, and I appreciate everything that you do for us."

The kids must have heard her voice because one by one with cake all over their faces, and ice cream all over their shirts, they ran into the kitchen screaming the word Mommy over and over again. Then she was attacked and stained by their hands, and this made her furious.

"What the hell is all this stuff on your faces and hands?" She glared at me, looking over her ruined new Gucci dress. It almost looked as if she wanted to cry.

I smiled at that. "Shift change!" I kissed her on the cheek and slipped out the door.

***

With the shower water spraying beads across my face I went over my inventory in my mind. I had less than a thousand dollars left to my name, and a little less than an eight ball of dope. I'd laid up with Amanda so long that I wasn't hustling. It was unlike me, but that's what young pussy was supposed to do to a man. I wasn't regretting my vacation, I was simply stating the obvious, so to speak.

After I was freshly dressed, I loaded my pipe and took a nice hard blast, inhaling until my chest felt like it was going to explode. I sent myself to paradise. This was some good ass dope, and for about ten minutes it took me away from my broken reality. I had to get on a move, and I had to do that shit immediately.

I dialed up Rallo and he picked up on the third ring. It sounded like he was blowing smoke out. "'Bout time you climb from between them young thighs and remembered who your people were."

"Rollo, meet me at my crib as soon as you can so we can talk business."

"Give me about an hour, and I'll be over there to put something on your brain just fine cat daddy."

"Alright. Solid, my man."

An hour later Rallo pulled up in a burgundy Cadillac Seville, clean. He stepped out fresh, with some fine threads on that made him look like a King Pin. He hugged me at the threshold then walked past, smelling like Gorgio Boutique.

"Damn, brotha, what you done did, robbed somebody else's lifestyle?" I joked, eyeing him from head to toe.

"Man, hell n'all. I'm about as broke as you probably are by now. You got something to smoke?" He licked his lips.

Same old Rallo, I thought. I threw him a twenty sack and watched him get his pipe and chore together. He looked so anxious and happy at the same time. He put flame to his piece and a big smile came across his face, holding in the smoke like it was the last of his life.

"So, what's with the car and the choice threads, Blood? You look like you done came up on a whole lot of something." I slumped on the couch across from him while he sat on the love seat.

He shook his head. "I wish, man. This comes from my old lady. I found myself a nice white lady that love black dick. So, in exchange for the said dick, she gave me most of her husband's old threads, and that's one of her cars out there that she let me roll around in as long as I check in with her and come whenever she call me."

I put fire to my rock and inhaled. I felt it overtake me and for a minute I couldn't help smiling. I was frozen. I set my paraphernalia on the table and sat back, letting the cloud take me away. I was feeling groovy. Damn this was some good ass dope. Rallo was still going on and on, but I tuned him out until he got the picture and finally shut up. I got up and made sure I locked the door. I checked out the window to make sure everything was cool on the block, then I checked the door again to make sure that I didn't unlock it instead of locking it. Once everything was confirmed and my high started to come down, I focused in on Rallo. He was lighting another piece and inhaling just as deeply as before. Then he was frozen.

"Man, what's up with Chicken? Where she been at?"

Rallo waved his hand through the air. "I don't know, man. Last time I saw her was two weeks ago on her way to the grocery store. She said she wasn't smoking no more dope and that she was changing her life for the better. Encouraged me to do the same."

"Damn, straight up? Aww, man, what's grooving with her? She must be back in that church and shit too, huh?"

He nodded. "She go three times a week up at that church on Sixty-third."

"Well you gotta respect that. It's plenty more fish in the sea." I laughed. "She fucked you up so bad she got you dating white women and all sorts of thangs."

He glared at me angrily. "Man, don't you know anything? You know anytime I'm fucking with a white broad it's gotta be for a specific reason. And this time ain't no damn different." He wiped the sweat from his forehead with his handkerchief. "Say, Blood, what you got to drink in here, my mouth drier than a desert in Nevada."

I came back and gave him a beer. "So, spill it, cat daddy. What's the make? What you got brewing with this old snow bunny, or is this a solo project that she don't know nothing about?"

He chugged the beer like he was in college at some sort of party. Then belched, neglecting to excuse his ill manners. I wondered if that was one of the reasons Chicken left his ass. That and probably his lack of respect for her. Same old Rallo. He had been this way ever since I'd met him. Old habits die hard I guessed. He was still my main-man, and nothing was gon' change that.

"The old broad hip. Her husband signed a prenuptial agreement when they first got married, and now he's trying to divorce her for a nineteen-year-old college girl. Her husband gotta be worth nearly a million dollars, but her lawyer told her the most she was due to get from him was a two thousand dollar alimony check every month, because they couldn't verify that he was really worth that much because he didn't use banks. He kept his money right in their very house, hidden in a safe."

This was starting to sound real fishy to me. "You mean to tell me that this broad want you to rob her husband and clean out his safe? Ain't that gon' seem odd, seeing as your black ass been sniffing around her white neighborhood already? And you driving her car, and wearing her husband's clothes? Don't you think that people gon' put two and two together? It didn't even take me that long, and they get paid to figure out that kind of shit."

Rallo was always doing something stupid. Now he was planning on pulling a caper on a white man while already fucking his wife. That was the stupidest shit I had ever heard. This joker had to be high as a muthafucka, and not from my dope.

"Peep this, Blood. Her husband don't mind that I'm fucking his wife. He actually had a part in hooking us up. They ain't had sex in years. She like black dick, and he like real young pussy. There is no dispute there. And he hasn't filed for divorce yet. He doesn't even know that she knows he's planning to divorce her. Far as he know, everything is kosher."

"I don't understand."

"She overheard him on the phone talking to his lawyer about possibly divorcing her. She just so happened to be walking down the hallway and eavesdropped on him in his study."

I shook my head. "I still think this a bad idea and you still ain't gave me no reason why it ain't."

He pulled out a Newport and lit it. "Her husband, Bruce, invited me to their poker game Friday. Julie— that's the white girl name— said he get real drunk during those poker games. She said he be slurring his words and falling all over, but he always goes into his study and counts his money every night, whether he drunk or sober. She said she don't know if he keep all his money there at the house, but she knows that his safe is in his study and that he makes a habit of most times falling asleep while the safe still open."

The more Rallo explained this lick, the more it confused me. This seemed like an easy enough take, I was wondering why he didn't go about knocking Julie's man off his self. Why was he trying to get me involved? I mean don't get me wrong, me and Rallo was thick as thieves. But I'd known him for more than twenty years, and I'd never known for him to split an easy take down the middle, especially when he could do it his self, which got me to wondering if it was more to it than he was telling me. I couldn't help being suspicious.

"Rallo, if this lick so damn easy, why didn't you just knock the husband off yourself, seeing that he gon' be drunk any damn way? Why would you decide to split things down the middle with me? Something ain't right about that." I walked to the kitchen, grabbed a beer, then came back and sat across from him. He was smoking up his last few pieces of dope. I allowed him to absorb the high for five minutes before I repeated all of my concerns and questions. By that time his head was together.

"Look, Blood, I'm gon' be partying with Bruce and a couple of his buddies, forcing the issue, trying to get them as drunk as possible. I'm gon' pretend to get so drunk that his three buddies that also coming along gon' need to drive me home way across town. It'll be during that time that you make your move and get Jim while he wasted. They can't blame it on me because they'll know they had to drop me off. And Julie can't get the blame because she is out of town with his sister for her wedding. The reason why I need you is so that it can be pulled off while I'm being escorted home. They don't know nothing about you."

"Man... What about the white bitch? Won't she know that it was you?" I lit a cigarette, mulling things over in my head. It seemed like it could go smooth, but that's how things always seemed when you planned them. What you could never factor in was how things would go once things didn't go according to plan.

Rallo waved his hand through the air dismissingly. "Don't worry about Julie, you let me take care of her. She ain't due back until next Sunday. She down in Kentucky. I might meet her down that way for a quick tryst. That way I can throw her off too."

Now I was confused. "Wait a minute, Rallo. I thought you said that she wanted you to rob his ass. If that's the case, then why would you go through great lengths to keep this from her? Say, Blood, something ain't right about this whole thang."

Large sweat beads started to break out on Rallo's forehead. He began to fidget and scratch the back of his neck. Then he lit another cigarette, even though he already had a half one smoking in the ash tray.

"Come off it, nigga, and tell me the real give with this move." I said tired of playing games.

"Damn, main-man, sometimes I hate how you know me so damn good. You just can't let me get away with nothing, can you?"

"Spill it, cat-daddy, and no more lies." I warned looking him directly in the eye.

"Alright, man, everything I told you is the truth with the exception of the old lady knowing about the robbery. He always count his money before he turn in like he don't trust his woman or something. I spent the night over there for a week straight, and every night it was the same routine. You have no idea how hard it was for me not knock his ass off the first few times. After ensuring that he did this every day that's when I formulated a plot to get his ass and her too 'cause she got plenty fine jewelry in that jewelry box of hers. All kinds of expensive earrings and bracelets and so on. It's all ensured, and she don't like most of it any damn way. True, she not hip to the robbery, but I'll take care of all of that, so don't you worry.

We gotta get that money before he do put it in the bank. That's why we gotta strike this Friday."

Now I was starting to get the gist. It was all starting to make sense. All Rallo had to do was tell me that in the first place, but getting the truth out of him was like getting a blind person to walk you across a busy street. We sat back for the next two hours planning the lick. I went over everything again and again until I was content that it would be smooth sailing.

That night after Rallo left, Amanda came downstairs beating on the door. The first thing she did when I let her in was sniff the air. Then she walked around the whole house inspecting it like she was my parole officer. After she was content, she stood in front of me and wrapped her slim arms around my neck.

"How are you baby?" She cooed in that addictive voice. She kissed me on the lips, then wiped her mouth. "Eww, you been smoking them nasty cigarettes again. You taste like an ashtray. Disgusting." She pointed a finger down her throat to emphasize her point, left and returned with a cap full of scope.

I put it in my mouth and gargled the spicy liquid. I swished it around in my mouth for thirty seconds, then spat in the toilet. She watched me the whole time smiling. Obviously amazed at how docile she had me. As soon as I wiped my mouth with a face towel, she was all over me, her tongue exploring every contour of my mouth.

I pulled back and stared down at her. "Amanda, what's the matter? Why you acting so frisky?"

She seemed hurt. "I thought you liked me being frisky, daddy. I guess you starting to get tired of me already. I knew that you would. I knew that eventually my children and my situation would run you off." She lowered her head in defeat. "I guess I'll see you when I see you, then." She made her way to the back door avoiding my eyes.

"Wait a minute, baby, you're tripping." I grabbed her and gave her three full minutes of tongue until she was panting and had her hand all the way inside my jeans and boxers, squeezing my manhood.

In one fluid motion she fell to her knees, unleashed me and speared her head on my Johnson until my toes curled.

I loved the way she looked me directly in the eye the whole time, stopping only to rub it all over her face. Then she was swallowing me again, taking me as deep as her throat allowed. When I came, I fell back against the wall in the kitchen while she continued to milk me. Before it was all said and done, I had her legs on my shoulders eating her like she was my last supper. She had a big clit that I sucked and nipped with my teeth until she was screaming at the top of her lungs. Then we were like animals, doggie style, her slamming back into me while I slammed forward with all of my might. We went at it for three hours straight, getting nastier and nastier each hour until we ended with me sexing her up against her front door after we were supposed to have been finished. I picked her up and made her slide down my pole until she climaxed, biting my bottom lip. She sucked me again and begged me to spend the night, but I declined.

Friday came so fast, but not fast enough. I was

basically broke, and by that time willing to do whatever it took to get my hands on some nice paper. I was down to two rocks and a hundred dollars, which meant I was in the red zone.

Rallo hit my line at ten-thirty. "What's up, mainman, you ready?"

I heard a bunch of ruckus in the background. It sounded like Sinatra was on the radio. I heard glasses clinking and laughter. "I'll be over there in twenty minutes, call me back at eleven sharp."

"Alright, man, hurry up."

I parked three blocks down and stayed within the shadows all the way till I got in front of the Victorian brick house. I was in all black, from ski mask to army boots. I was armed with a .38 Special, which I was hoping I didn't have to use. I also had my army knife as well in case I had to pry some information. My hip began to vibrate; it was Rallo.

"Where you at, main-man?"

"Here." I crouched on the side of the house and slid to the backyard, laying low. From my vantage point I could hear the music coming from the inside. The lights were dimmed, but you could tell that they were having a gay old time.

"Alright, man, the backdoor is open. Give me about twenty minutes and I'ma pass out and tell them to take me home. After that, everything should fall into place accordingly."

I hung up then slid down with my back to the house. The neighborhood was quiet with the exception of a few dogs barking a couple houses down. They had a big pool in their backyard, with a table with an umbrella over it to shade the sun. Around the table were four chairs. To my left was a big, expensive barbeque grill. These people were definitely well off. I got to imagining me living in this house and not having a care in the world. I was so absorbed within my own head that I had not noticed the music stopped. I snapped out of my zone when I heard a car engine turn over in the front of the house. Then I heard country ass Rallo saying his goodbyes and that he would be back next Friday to win his money back. His words were slurred. After that, more goodbyes, then the car drove off and it was quiet.

I waited another fifteen minutes before I tried the back door. To my amazement, Jim had not locked it yet. I twisted the knob and slowly slipped into the house. The sounds of Sinatra filled my ears, I could smell pizza, and that made my stomach growl. Once again, I went the whole day without eating something. Sometimes it was so hard to remember.

The back door opened to a pair of stairs. One set would take you upstairs, and the other would take you to the basement. I chose the flight that took me upstairs and right into the kitchen. The house was dark, so it was real hard to make out anything. I closed my eyes, then re-opened them, trying to adjust to the darkness. The trick worked because at least then I was able to see the outline of things.

I mentally followed the directions me and Rallo had gone over. *When you come into the kitchen, make a left and walk straight until you see a fireplace.* I saw it. *Once you see the fireplace, take a right out of that den and follow the hallway until you see a bathroom. The door will be open with a bright light.* I saw that too. *At the bathroom turn to your left and you should see Jim sitting in his study, hopefully counting his money...* Well what do you know...

I stood outside of the study watching the Robert De Niro looking man taking stacks of money out of his safe and placing them on his desk. Once they were all piled on, he took a stack at a time placing them into a safe that looked like a mini refrigerator. I could not believe how on point Rallo was. He must have done some serious plotting.

I threw caution to the wind. I walked right into the study and flashed the .38. "Freeze, mother-fucker!" I did my best to sound white. "You son-of-a- bitch, if you move one muscle I'm going to bust a cap in your ass."

He threw his hands way up in the sky. "Please, don't shoot. Go ahead, you can take the money. Just don't shoot."

"Take off that robe," I hissed

"What?"

"Motherfucker, you heard me, I said take off that robe and wrap all that money up in it!"

He slung the robe off of his shoulders and began to do exactly what I said. I looked around the study for anything else of value. It was full of old books and European art. He wrapped the money, then handed it to me and I grabbed it. "Okay, pal, you have the money. Now just leave my house, please?"

I was intending to do just that when I heard, "Jim, who are you talking to? Don't tell me you're – Ahhh! Oh my God!"

"Bitch, shut the fuck up!" I grabbed her by the neck and threw her into the study. She was a blonde, about 19 years old, real pretty; not my type though.

She had on so much jewelry it was like she was playing dress up. I imagined she'd went upstairs and put on all of Julie's jewelry to make a statement. "Who else is in this house?" I demanded.

She was the first to speak. "Just us, please don't kill us. Please, I'm still in college."

"You got the money, friend. Please leave." Jim pleaded.

They were terrified, and I was panicking. If I left them like they were I would be caught in ten minutes. I had to come up with something quick. First, I had to get all that jewelry that the blonde had on. I looked down and saw that beside Jim's desk was a small garbage can. I ordered the woman to dump the garbage out and to take the plastic bag that once held the contents of paper and other miscellaneous items, and put all of her jewelry inside of it. She rushed, throwing all of the jewelry in the bag as if it were burning hot to her skin. Without being told she reached and pulled off Jim's watch, which was a Rolex, and threw it into the bag along with his wedding ring. I was impressed. It was like this wasn't her first time. She even gave me a sultry look after she finished the tasks. It was if the threat of danger was somehow turning her on. I smiled beneath my mask.

After tying them to each other, back to back, with a thick roll of duct tape Jim had helped me locate, I rummaged through the house, locating the rest of the jewelry. I took that. I'd also found Jim's gun case. He had so many rifles and shotguns that it was amazing the robbery had went as smooth as it had. I took all of them. It took me ten minutes to get back to my car. I drove home so paranoid; I just knew that I wasn't gon' make it.

Hood Rich

Chapter 4
Binkey

I had been out the hospital for two months, and I still felt sick. I couldn't believe I almost lost my son, and that in the process I also almost lost my own life. By the grace of God my son was about 95 percent healthy now. Jaheim Husane. We had given him Barack Obama's middle name but spelled it with an A instead of an E. The pigs didn't wait long to get me out of that so-called lap of luxury in the hospital before they slapped me back in Cook County Jail awaiting charges of double homicide. I was sick and had already lost fifteen pounds. I just couldn't bring myself to eat the garbage that they were serving on a daily. I had this major thing about cleanliness, and that was something that this jail wasn't. I had never seen so many rats and cockroaches until I got here. The water was damn near gray, and sometimes it turned brown when you ran it for a lengthy period of time. The guards were careless and just as gangsta as the convicts they housed. I got hit on more times by them I had probably been hit on by men in my whole life. It was like they craved jail pussy.

They put me in a cell block where every woman was there for murder, or multiple murders. Everybody in our block was facing life sentences. Most of the women paced with looks of despair written across their faces, while others never came out of their cells. Some looked so crazy that I often felt my flesh crawl when they walked past me. It was about seventy-five of us in this division and out of that number, I would only say that ten of us seemed as if we were normal.

I was originally one of the females that never came out of my room, but then I started to think about my son and Roman, and these charges against me. Before I knew it, they were cutting into me so bad that I just had to get up and get out. So, I started out by pacing. Then I tried the exercise route, because every day we were allowed a few hours of gym. So, I'd go there and run around or jump rope until I began to feel nauseous from my lack of eating. I quickly stopped going to the gym, especially after two broads got stabbed up. I never found out why it happened, I just knew that I wasn't messing with that gym no more. I didn't like the way most of the women looked at me anyway, so there was no telling when they'd try and do something to me. I was alone, without my trusted machete, and outnumbered.

Roman wrote me short letters every day that I still neglected to answer. I still hadn't forgiven him for getting that Kelly chick pregnant. Then she ain't make it no better by calling the police on me and getting me into this terrible predicament. But then again, if she had not, Roman would have been dead right now, and her ass was next. So maybe she did do the right thing. I guess only God knows.

In addition to not returning his letters, I was also not excepting his visits. I didn't know if I wanted anything to do with him anymore, or if I still needed time to heal. Apart of me missed him, and I worried about him every single day. I missed his handsome dark brown face, with his deep waves that were always shining, his lining always crisp. He always smelled so good, and walked with an air of confidence I had never known until him. I missed his breath, I missed feeling his strong arms being wrapped around me, and to be honest I even missed how he felt when he entered my body.

I did want to see him, but I felt that seeing him would only make me feel worst because he would be leaving my life all over again every time they took me away in chains. So, I was all alone and facing the worst charges possible.

I was sitting on my bunk with my head down, trying to give myself a reason to cheer up, when the bailiff came to my cell and told me that I had a visitor. To be ready, that they would be taking me down in ten minutes. I perked up. I wanted to ask him who the visitors were, but at that point I was hoping it was Roman. I started to break down from just imagining his face. I hurried and washed up as best I could in the small metal sink that was attached to the toilet. After I felt that I 'd made myself as presentable as I possibly could, I took a deep breath and allowed them to escort me to the visiting window booths. They told me my visitors were in booth seven. I took another deep breath and approached the place where he pointed. When I got there, I saw Heaven sitting in front of the window with tears in her eyes, already holding the phone.

My heart started to skip beats. *Oh my God, something has happened to Roman. What could have possibly taken place?* I was so scared that I didn't pick up the phone for three full seconds. When I did, I placed it to my ear.

"Heaven, girl, what's the matter? Please tell me that ain't nothing happen to Roman!" I screamed into the phone. I was beside myself. I had some of the worst images going through my mind.

Heaven shook her head. "N'all, girl, Roman alright. These tears in my eyes are for you. You don't call nobody. You turn down all your visits. You don't accept the attorney. Binkey, what is the matter with you? What are you trying to do to us? Especially my brother." She looked distraught as if she'd been crying for the last few nights. I never thought she cared about me this much.

I shrugged. "Heaven, I don't know. I guess my heart is hurt ever since I found out he got Kelly pregnant. I just been feeling some type of way about life. Like I just want to be alone. Roman hurt me, girl." I felt the tears coming down my cheeks, at the same time my stomach growled.

"Little sister, I understand that one hundred percent. But do you understand that he is not the only one that love you? You are my sister, girl. I been knowing you since before you had your first period. Do you remember who gave you advice about how to properly take care of your cycle?"

I nodded. "You."

"You damn right it was me. Now you and Roman going through a rough time, but that doesn't mean that you go and withdraw into yourself, and say screw the rest of the family. How do you expect to see Jahiem while you in here? How do you expect to be a part of his life if you shut off the whole family?" She dabbed her eyes with a tissue. "You got Roman out here living Kamikaze. The boy ain't right. He don't stay in no place too long. He smoking that gas one blunt after the other. He started to drink, and his temper is the worst I have ever seen it. I have never seen him act this way before over no woman. So, if you think that boy don't love you, you are crazy. If he get his self locked up or killed, then what? What is y'all son supposed to do? What about Mya?"

What she was saying was making so much sense. I knew Roman, and he was not good with handling broken emotions. He had still not gotten over his mother's death. I guess I was his refuge with that. Now that I'm gone, it had to feel like a second death to him. Maybe I was going about things all wrong. "Sister, you're right. I think I might be acting somewhat selfish. It ain't right for me to put my own feelings before the welfare of my son and his father. Lord knows I really love y'all more than my next breath. But I'm fucked!" I was crying hard by this time. "They say they got my knife with two men DNA on it that's been murdered. They want to pin the murders on me. I refuse to talk to any detectives, so they decided to screw me over. I don't even know what they talking about." I lied. "I found that knife and just kept it."

"Then, sister, let us get you the best damn attorney money can buy, and get you the fuck out of here. You don't belong in here and we don't want you in here. Please say you'll take the attorney." Her eyes poured into mine, pleading.

My heart softened. "Okay."

When I got back to the block the guard handed me three envelopes. Two were addressed from Roman and one was addressed from Rihanna. I was shocked. It said:

Dear Binkey,
Girl, I know we ain't never really been the best of

friends, but I wanted you to know that I am here for you. You are the mother of my daughter's brother, and Mya loves you. She talks about you all the time and wants to know if she can write to you and send you pictures of Jaheim.

I don't know if you will respond or not but if you do, I will write you back. I am sending you $100.00 for your commissary account. Whether you write back or not I'll send you this every month. Take care, a friend.

Rihanna

That letter had me somewhat emotional because I had forgotten about the impact my situation would have on Mya. I didn't want to hurt her, and I respected Rihanna for being the woman that she was. I wasn't sure if I could have done the same if the tables were turned. I would think hard as to whether I would write her back or not.

I braced myself, sitting on my bunk. I checked the postmark dates and opened the first letter that Roman mailed out to me. It read:

Precious Goddess,

May Allah's blessings be upon you. It's been months and you still ain't trying to give me the time of day. No matter how many letters I send to you apologizing for what went on between me and Kelly, you seem like you just won't let the BS go... I really don't know what else to do, or what else to say. Our son is beautiful, just like you. Every time I look at him, I see you, and that breaks me down and that's usually when I wind up writing you another letter, since you don't call or except my visits. I just want you to know that you breaking me down. I'm losing it and I'm starting to get careless, Goddess. You got me changing niggas left and right and not even accepting bread for it. My heart hurts. I know I'm supposed to be standing up and taking care of our son, but every time I look at him all I see is you, and I break the fuck down. I need you, B. I love you, I swear I do. Anyway, Heaven and my Grandmother been holding Jaheim down while I'm getting my mind together. I don't know what tomorrow holds, but you ain't here, so it don't matter anyway. I always thought that you would be my wife.

Allah knows best,

Roman

Tears were pouring down my eyes so bad that I got up and grabbed the tissue before I opened his second letter. As soon as I did, multiple pictures fell out. I laid them face-down on the bed without even looking at them because I wanted to enjoy them later. I began reading his second letter as the guard came to my cell.

"Ms. Green, are you eating dinner?" He boomed.

"No, I'm okay, thank you."

He looked me up and down before leaving.

Precious Goddess,

May Allah's blessings be upon you... I'm tired of hurting, and I'm tired of living without you. I got a lot of stuff on my mind, and only one remedy that's gon' get 'em off. I don't give a fuck about me no more. You were my better half. I got some shit lined up, and I hope I don't make it back. Your actions have already changed me over, so what does it matter if it happens in the physical. I just want you to know that I loved you, and that you are the first female that I ever cared about. I always thought that you would be my wife. I fucked that up. Jaheim gon' be straight. I made sure of that. And I'm gon' make sure you get at least a hundred dollars every two weeks until they let you out of there. I might not see you again, but I will live on through my seeds. Who knows, maybe this just the liquor talking. I miss you though, boo. You got me all fucked up.

Roman

PS... These are flicks of our son.

I cried and laid his letter to the side, flicking through the pictures one by one. I could not believe how handsome our son really was. Roman held him in different poses. Some pictures were of Mya holding him. His hair was already growing in fully. His dimples were prominent.

It was at that moment that I snapped out of it. What the fuck was I doing? Was I really willing to throw my life away, throw my son away, throw Roman away, just because he made a mistake? I had to be crazy.

That night after the day room opened back up, I called somebody collect for the first time since I had been in. Heaven accepted the call. "Girl, I can't believe you calling. It's a miracle! Praise the Lord! Have mercy!" she shouted.

I couldn't help but laugh. I knew that even though she was being funny that parts of her reaction was authentic. I composed myself, then grew serious. "Heaven, how are you doing?"

"I'm fine. I talked to your new attorney today and he said he'd be out there first thing Monday morning. He promises to get you out of there. Them people wishing on a star."

I surely hope she was right. "Where is Roman?" I blurted out before she ended her sentence good enough.

She paused. "Sis, I haven't heard from him in two days."

Hood Rich

Chapter 5
Roman

I ain't ever tooted powder a day in my life. Here I was sitting at the table at Chicken's house with four thick lines separated on top of a dinner plate. I was already knocking back Remy Martin and smoking blunt after blunt. My head was fucked up. I was hurting, and I'd heard a long time ago that cocaine numbs you to all pains. Well, I was seconds away from finding out before I heard the front door open.

I upped both chrome automatic .45's, and pointed them in the direction of the noise. When Chicken walked in carrying two paper grocery bags, my heart started beating so fast. But clearly hers didn't. When she saw the two guns she dropped the bags and screamed out loud before slapping a hand over her mouth.

"Roman! What the hell are you doing here? How did you get into my house?" She picked the bags back up, walking into the kitchen and setting them on the table. She had on a form-fitting dark blue dress. Her natural, pretty hair flowed across her shoulders, and her scent was Chanel. I stood up in front of her. She looked at me as if she were afraid. "Boy, what's the matter? Are you alright?"

Before she could say anything else, I picked her up. As if on instinct she wrapped her legs around my waist and our lips met, then tongues. I carried her into the living room and sat her down. She stood on the tips of her toes, sucking on my lips and trying to get my shirt over my head. I slapped her hands away and bent her over the arm of the couch, pulling her dress up to her hips. I exposed a pair of light blue bikini cut panties. In one yank I snatched them off and spread her legs apart.

She looked back at me over her shoulder. "Do it to me, son. Do momma good. Please, baby, I need it so damn bad!" Her hand slid between her legs and opened the lips to her sex.

I slid the Magnum on and slid into her wetness.

She groaned. "Damn, boy, that's too much dick for one man to have. Oh my god, it feel so damn good, baby."

I fucked her with anger, trying to take all of my sorrows away. She slammed back on me as if she were equally mad. Her tightness squeezing me and trying to milk me of my seed. I grabbed her pretty hair and yanked her head back, making her back arch, allowing me to dig as deep as necessary.

Her moaning sounded throughout the whole house. That and the slapping of our skins. "Yes, baby, yes, yes, do me right, Roman! Oh! Fuck!"

She started trembling, then shaking. All at once she screamed and fell to the floor with me on top of her ass still plunging a mile a second. I lifted her left leg up and went to work. Digging into her wetness until I exhausted myself which was two hours later.

Afterward, I laid back while she kissed and sucked all over my body. My mind was somewhere else. All I could think about was Binkey and our newborn son. I didn't know how I was gon' live out here without my right hand. To me, shorty was more than just my baby momma. She was my purpose.

Few hours later, the four powder lines were sitting back in front of me at the kitchen table. I couldn't bring myself to fuck with that shit. I had seen it destroy too many of my loved ones in its rock form. I ain't wanna take that chance.

Chicken came from behind me while I was sitting down and slid her chin onto my shoulder. "Baby, you know you ain't gon' do that dope. You might as well put that stuff back up because that ain't you." She kissed me on the check and went back to frying the chicken on the stove. "What you need to do is sit down and have a nice dinner with me. Calm your mind and stop letting the stress of the world get to you. You gotta let go and let God."

I put the powder back in the Ziplock bag with the rest of the four ounces I had taken off some random nigga that I had also changed over. Didn't even think twice, just pulled up on him on 26th and North Avenue, he came to the stolen car I was driving and asked me if I wanted some candy. I nodded. He jumped in the passenger seat, and I blew his brains all against the passenger window soon as he closed the door. I took his dope, though I wasn't worried because I never took my gloves off. Then I left his ass there to rot.

Two days before that, I caught two police officers going into the Dunkin Donuts on Cottage Grove. I ran up on them, masked, and pumped four shots a piece in each one of their faces then ran.

That was three people in two days, and I was still feeling just as sick as I was before I changed them. My head was fucked up. I was starting to miss my mother again, and I didn't think I was fit to be around my newborn while I was feeling like this. I hadn't seen him in four days, and even though I was missing him like crazy, I wasn't ready to see him or Mya yet.

I came over to Chicken's house one day last week after I had changed over these two Mexican studs that kept mugging me at the gas station. She accepted me with open arms at three in the morning, and I respected her for that. Tonight was the first night that we ever fucked around. Prior to that she had only referred to me as her son. But after watching that sexy ass body roam around for damn near two weeks straight, I just had to get me a taste. Her femininity was so sexy. I think it was also the fact that she catered to me like a son that also made me attracted to her. Sounds weird, but it is what it is.

She bent over and checked on the cornbread. By this time, she'd showered and changed into her black, form-fitting, laced night gown, showcasing her sexy upper thighs. She spoke from the side of her face without looking over to me.

"And, sugar, what got into you? Umm! Boy, any time you wanna tame this pussy you come right ahead. You took me back a few years with all them inches. Damn, you gifted!" She shook her head. "Now I'm gon' put some food in your stomach. You starting to get a little thin. Momma don't like that."

I definitely was hungry, but at the same time I didn't have an appetite. I couldn't keep nothing down. And I knew that I was losing weight, but that wasn't really a major factor to me. I would bounce back once I got my head together. I was sure of that.

"And, son, why you been so quiet?" She turned around looking at me for the first time. She reached and put the back of her hand on my forehead. "Are you sick? Don't feel like it. What's the matter?" She gave me concerned eyes and smiled weakly.

I shook my head, expressionless. "I'm good, Chicken. I just gotta get my head together. I got a lot on my mind." I took another swig from the Remy Martin bottle. My high and buzz had long gone, so I was starting to feel the pain again of my reality.

She sat down next to me and pulled her chair closer, patting my thigh. "You know I'm here if you wanna talk about it right? Whatever you need from me, all you have to do is let me know."

I nodded. "I know, but like I said I'm good though." I picked up her hand and kissed the back of it. "You betta stop worrying about me so much. I don't want you falling all in love and shit." I attempted a smile.

"Chile, after what you just put on me, I ain't far from it." She waved her hand through the air, then got up to check on the cornbread in the oven. "So, you gon' eat with me tonight, or am I gon' be eating by my lonesome?" She sounded weary and sad.

"I got some business to take care of, then I'll be back to spend the night if you want me to."

She pulled the cornbread out of the oven and placed it on a warmer. Then she stirred the pot of collard greens, checked on the pinto beans and white rice. "Son, that sounds good to me, but what time are you planning on getting back? You know what? Doesn't matter." She paused, looking me over. "You got your key?"

I nodded.

***

Heaven had been blowing up my phone all week and not once did I have the decency to call her back.

I figured that as long as she was calling that everything was good. All of her messages just said that she was worried about me and wondering where I was. So, I didn't feel like there was any rush to get back to her. Like I said, my head was fucked up. My best friend and son's mother was facing a double homicide, and the bitch that I had gotten pregnant was the one that called the police and put her there.

I slid up to Heaven's door unannounced and rang the doorbell. The porch light came on, then the door swung open. My nephew rushed me and wrapped his arms around me. He was getting tall. He had to be almost 5'7".

"Uncle Roman! Man, what's good? Where you been at?" He whispered, "You know my momma mad at you."

Before he could finish giving me the 411, Heaven appeared at the door. "Tarig, go to your room." She ordered while looking me in the eyes.

"Yes, ma'am." He turned and walked away with his head down. "I love you, Uncle Roman.

"I love you too, nephew." I avoided eye contact with Heaven, even though I felt hers piercing into me.

She grabbed me by the arm and pulled me into the house. "Boy, get yo' ass in here!" She demanded.

I sat on the couch and started to explain myself. She shushed me and told me to hold on, then pointed toward Tarig Junior's room. She walked over to her big sound system, and then I heard Keith Sweat pouring out, *"I will never do anything to hurt you."*

She came and sat on the couch next to me. "I didn't want Tarig to hear what we talking about because

I'm getting ready to tear into your ass." Her face frowned up, then she reached and pulled my ear like our mother used to do. Getting very close, she growled in my ear, "Roman, do you have any idea how worried sick I been over you? You been missing for damn near two weeks straight, and you ain't even had the time to call me and let me know that you were okay! How dare you treat me like I'm one of your little hoe's? I am your sister. I thought I was the one person in life that you truly cared about, yet you allow me to mentally suffer, worrying about whether you are alive or not." Through clenched teeth she said, "Now explain to me where you been, and what's been going on!"

She released my ear and I didn't even have enough nerve to frown at her. I respected Heaven as the second coming of my mother. She was my heart. I could never disrespect her or lie to her just like I couldn't my mother.

I gazed into her angry eyes, and for some reason mine glazed up. "Sis, I feel like I'm losing my mind." A tear fell. "I'm fucking up, Heaven. I'm missing Momma, and now I done lost the one female who I actually really cared about. I'm missing my son, but I'm afraid to be around him because my mind ain't right."

"You been killing again?" She said this lowly.

I nodded. "I can't help it. Every time them feelings start getting the best of me, I feel like I gotta change somebody. I got so much anger and frustration within me."

She wiped a tear that was falling down my cheek. "I know, Roman. You haven't been eating either, have you?" By this time tears were falling down her cheeks.

I shook my head. "I ain't had no appetite, and when I do try to eat something, I wind up throwing it back up." I felt a lump developing in my throat. I couldn't stop the tears from coming down my cheeks. I felt like I was losing it.

Heaven wrapped her arms around my neck and kissed my cheek. "It's going to be okay, Roman. We'll get through this. I promise."

The song switched over on the Keith Sweat CD. *"You may be young but you're readdddy."* He belted out.

"I miss Binkey, Heaven."

She jerked up. "Speaking of which, guess what?"

I turned to her pretty face. "What?"

"I went to see her the other day and she missing you just as much. She told me that she want to see you, and that she going to accept the lawyer. Roman, she want to come home to you. Y'all gon' be alright. That girl still love you."

I was feeling a lil' better all of the sudden. "You think so? You think she over Kelly being pregnant?"

Heaven scrunched her face. "Boy, now you know that as a woman she will never get over that. But I know that she ready to fight for her family. I saw the longing in her eyes, and I heard it in her voice when she called over here looking for you the other day. What you need to do is to go down there and see that girl. Y'all need to grow up and to get a better under-standing as adults." She laid her head on my chest. "Oh, and hold on." She jumped up. A minute later she returned with Jahiem wrapped in his blue baby blanket. "This is why you need to get your tail down there." She handed him to me.

I held him in my arms and my whole life flashed before my eyes. I searched over his whole face. He was an angel. Handsome and a reflection of me and Binkey. At that moment I knew that I had to fight for my family.

The phone rang. "Here, Roman, it's for you, it's Charles."

"Charles?" I was confused.

"You know, Champ."

Hood Rich

Chapter 6
Roman

"Bro, I gotta see you right now, it's urgent!"

I'd forgotten all about Champ. I had so much going on that I neglected to pursue lil' D's murder investigation. I didn't forget about her, and would definitely get back to it. It's just that my head wasn't right. "Say, Champ, what's this pertaining?"

There was a long pause on the phone before he answered. "It's better if we discuss this in person. I ain't gon' say it over the phone."

I got his message loud and clear. I kissed my son on the forehead and handed him back to Heaven. She gave me a look of concern, then started to rock Jaheim. I got up preparing to leave.

"What did he have to say, Roman?" She narrowed her eyes at me. She looked disappointed and a little bit irritated. Bouncing the baby slightly up and down with his chest against her shoulder, she patted him softly on the pamper. "Well?"

"Business, Heaven." I leaned over and pecked her on the cheek. "I'll be back tomorrow, don't worry. Tell my nephew that I love him and that I'll see him tomorrow after he get home from school."

I kissed her again and left out the door with her shaking her head. I pulled up in the parking lot of Bottoms Up Tavern. Soon as I pulled in, I saw Champ's truck. When he saw my whip, he jumped out of his truck and slid into my passenger seat. The parking lot was empty with the exception of three other cars. It was only a little after 8, and Bottoms Up didn't even open until 10.

The parking lot sat in the darkness, next to an alley. Across the street were abandoned buildings and a strip where prostitutes strolled. They didn't pay us no mind, and we didn't pay them any either. I made sure I stayed on point. This area was running by the Essays, and they were known to creep up on you something fierce, which is why I had parked so that my vision was toward their buildings, and the prostitutes were in my rearview. I adjusted my .40 Glock in my waist and turned down that old school Tupac "All Eyez on Me". No matter what went on in life, that CD was always on point and had a track on there that preached about the struggle you were going through. I scanned the scenery again and checked my rearview mirror. A yellow sista was getting into a john's car, they quickly pulled off, then it was calm behind us, but I still kept checking back and forth.

"So, what's good, joe?" I turned looking at Champ. He had on a black hoodie with the hood pulled over his head. That looked suspicious to me, and it kinda put me on edge. I nonchalantly slid my hand closer to my waistband. The .40 was already off safety. This nigga was giving me a bad vibe.

He acted as if he didn't notice my movements. "You remember I told you that I was gon' check into the history behind Moeshe sending us on that move to Milwaukee?"

I nodded.

"Well, it turns out that it's just like you said. That nigga JJ sent us up there to get changed over. Moeshe said that he ain't do business with them niggas from Milwaukee no more because the last lil' delivery men he'd sent up that way had been robbed, and them same niggas swore up and down that they didn't have nothing to do with it. Moeshe demanded his money or his work from them niggas, but their only retort was to say fuck him. Turns out JJ got family that still live up that way, and on that same block. When I told Moeshe what happened, he had JJ snatched up and interrogated. After losing his kneecaps to Big Hurk, who smashed them in with a hammer, JJ spilled everything. I guess I should have told you that a few years ago I knocked him out over cursing in front of my mother. Me and him have had bad blood ever since then. He told Moeshe that those cats we changed over was constantly robbing his lil' brothers and shooting up his mother's house. That nigga sent us up to Milwaukee as a bargaining tool. Them studs demanded four kilos to leave his people alone. So, he set it up that we make that delivery. He told the niggas that if they changed us, he would send down twenty gees the following week. Had you not acted when you did, we'd a been dead, bro."

I was clenching my jaw so hard it was starting to hurt. I knew I had a feeling. One thing about being a killer is that you always know when the angel of death is around. It's like y'all get an understanding— the angel knows when it's your time, but it also lets you know when its present just to give you a heads up that your time is getting closer, telling you that for now, make me happy and you do that by murdering what the angel had come for.

"Bro, I already knew. I ain't never trusted JJ. What's good with him now? Where he at?"

Champ took his finger and drug it across his

neck. "I murdered that coward with Moeshe's blessing. And guess what?"

"What's that?"

"He made me his right hand man, and I'm making you mine. But look, bro. I don't want you as my partner in dealing with this heroin shit. N'all, my nigga. I want you strictly to change ma'fuckas over that's in my way. I am sure that we can get the proper price on the table. Bro, you saved my life. I wanna repay you, and I wanna make sure that you keep looking after me. What do you think?"

Chapter 7
Scooby

"Nigga, this yours right here." I pushed $250,000 across the table to Rallo and watched as his eyes bugged out of his head. It was half of the $500,000 that was in the safe.

He started slobbering at the mouth and rubbing his eyes. "Main-man, you sure all of this is mine? I ain't gotta cut nobody else in?" He said this talking from the side of his face. The whole time his eyes didn't leave the money. His hands were shaking. He pulled out his cigarettes, popped one out of the Newport box and put it up to his trembling lips. He dropped the lighter twice trying to light it.

"Say, man, get a whole of yourself, jive turkey. That there is your cut. You can do anything with it that you please. You cut somebody in, that's your thang. Me? I ain't got nothing to do with that." I eyed him closely as he continued to shake as if he was having a mild seizure. He shook so hard that ashes dropped all over his shirt.

He put down that cigarette, which was half gone and lit another one, dropped the lighter again, then knocked over the ashtray. He bent down to pick it up, bumped his head on the table, then stood up with a growing knot on his forehead. "Say, main- man, boy, this here is quite the lick. I can't even contain myself." By this time, he was sweeping up the ashes into the dustpan. "You know we gotta throw ourselves a party. I'm gon' invite every foxy momma in the Windy City, young and old. And we gon' have us a pajama party. That way, I can dig into some fine cat.

Everything is on me. I'ma get a whole kilo just to smoke. I want it powder too, that way I can cut it up myself so I can knock these foxes' socks off. Man, I'ma barbeque some ribs. Pork! Pork ribs! 'Cause I feel too good to eat beef. I want some swine, and some spaghetti, and all the trimmings. Man, I'm gon' try and get Chicken to come over and throw down! Two hundred and fifty thousand! I'm Ghetto rich, bitch!" He started dancing around, waving his arms in the air and stomping his feet.

I couldn't believe this fool. He was doing everything that he swore to me he wouldn't do. Rallo's crazy ass just never understood or saw the big picture. I had a feeling he was gon' be my downfall one day.

"Say, Blood, I ain't gon' be able to make it to your party 'cause I got some things to do outta town. I'm probably gon' be away for a few weeks. But I wish you all the best."

He stopped dancing and turned to me with a sick expression on his face. "Come on, Scooby. Why every time we strike it big you always gotta spoil it by not being a part of the celebration? Last time we hit, I ain't see you until the money was gone. What's the matter with you, man?" He started grabbing stacks of money and throwing them into a book bag that he'd brought with him. Occasionally, he would glare at me angrily.

"Rallo, you just don't get it do you? You a plum fool, ain't you?" I shook my head. "You set to be the number one suspect after all this shit done happened, now you finna go around town advertising that you ghetto rich, tricking on a whole lot of pussy and smoking thirty-six ounces of dope. Throwing a party instead of laying your ass low. Fool, you gon' get your ass locked up. I ain't gon' be nowhere around when you do. Fuck that, if I'm gon' get locked up, it's gon' be by my own fuck up, not because of the stupid shit you planning." I waved him off. "I gotta lot of love for you, baby, but you just dumb some times."

Rallo finished loading up his book bag and nodded. "I told you I got this under control." He glared.

* * *

Two days later I moved out of that duplex and found me another low-key spot on the Northside, right on Sheraton Boulevard. It was an area that was mostly senior citizens. There were a few fools around, but for the most part the area was cool. Two restaurants were on the corner— a McDonald's and a KFC. Across the street from them was a laundry mat, and a cashier's exchange and liquor store. Everything was less than half a block away, and that was perfect for me. The night before, I'd argued with Amanda for damn near two hours straight.

"Why you gotta move all the way to the Northside? Who you trying to run away from Scooby?" She stood in front of me with her hand on her hip. "What, you trying to run away from me and the boys? You don't want to be a part of us no more?"

This particular day I didn't feel like arguing, I was trying to get so much done, and I was trying to get done with everything within those 48 hours that I was set to move out. She'd caught the movers loading my furniture into their truck. We were in the kitchen, and every time that I tried to leave, she kept blocking my way.

"Amanda, get out my way, girl, so I can make sure don't none of these people steal none of my shit." I continued to look over her shoulder at the Spanish movers.

"Fuck them! Don't nobody wanna steal none of that old stuff you got, and I know damn well that you don't care about that shit either. You just avoiding my questions. Now I ain't finna get out of your way until you tell me what's going on. Are you trying to escape me and my children, or what?" She continued to stand in my way, glaring at me with her hand on her hip.

"Girl, what's the matter with you? The last two weeks you done spent more time at the mall than the people who work there. I done furnished your whole house, filled up your kids' wardrobes and yours, and got you a car. If I was trying to run away from your ass, don't you think I would have done it before I spent all of that money?"

She lowered her head in embarrassment, then stomped her feet. "I guess you're right, baby, but I still don't want you to leave me. I done already fell in love with you." She said, barely above a whisper. When she looked back up at me there were tears in her eyes.

I had heard enough. I felt like this girl thought I was going off to another planet or something when I was only moving to a different side of town. I had just bought her a brand-new Jeep Grand Cherokee. If she wanted to see me, she knew how to drive to come and get to me.

"Amanda, you overreacting, lil' momma. You acting like I'm moving out of Chicago. I ain't but twenty minutes away. I ain't giving up on you or those kids. Don't you know that I'm a better man than that? I —" I began.

"Scooby, I'm pregnant with your baby." She said it so low that I couldn't even hear her.

"What did you just say?"

She had her head bowed as if she had done something wrong. Her diamond earrings sparkled when she turned back up to face me. "I said, I'm pregnant with your baby and I'm freaking out because I don't know what to do. My sons' father will be home shortly, and I know he ain't gon' take this too kindly. But at the same time, I done fell in love with you, but I don't know how you feel about me, and I'm pregnant. And it's with your baby. Now you're moving, and I got your baby inside of me and I'm just freaking out, and it's all your fault." Tears poured down her cheeks.

I was stumped. I didn't know what to say or do. My stomach kept flipping over and over again. I looked down on this beautiful young girl and had so many mixed feelings going on inside of me. What the hell was I gon' do with a newborn at my age and by a young girl that already had two kids by a man that was on his way home? What had I gotten myself into?

"Amanda, how did this happen? I thought you was on some kind of pill or something." I asked dryly.

"How did this happen? How did this happen? Nigga, you fucked me damn near fifty times and you might have used protection twice! What you thought, 'cause you were older that you couldn't get women pregnant no more? Umm, I'm sorry, it don't work like that, so you gon' need a better response than 'How did this happen'." Her chest rose and fell. Her nostrils flared in anger. She gave me the look of death, like if I didn't say the right words in the next few seconds that she would kill me. "Go ahead, Scooby, I'm listening." She snapped.

I nudged past her, reached into the refrigerator and pulled out the gallon of milk jug that I had filled with water three days ago. For some reason, this new revelation made my throat dry. I popped the cap and turned it up taking long swallows. I was drinking so fast that most of the water spilled down the front of my shirt and spilled to the floor. I guess a part of me was trying to avoid the inevitable with Amanda.

Her hand still placed on her hip she balanced her weight from one foot to the next. I could tell that she was growing angrier and angrier. "Scooby, you can stand there all day long faking like you drinking that stale ass water, but I know damn well all you doing is trying to get your thoughts together. Nigga, you is not slick. Ugh!" She stormed out the kitchen and plopped down on the sofa the movers were intending on moving next.

They gave me a look of irritation. I held up one finger.

Kneeling in front of her, I rubbed one of her knees. "Amanda, you need to calm down, lil' lady. You know I'm gon' do everything that I can for you. Look, we can go down to the clinic tomorrow and get this situation taken care of."

Her head jerked back, eyes popped open. She smacked her hand off of her knee. "What did you just say? Scooby, I swear I know you didn't just say what I think you did." She stood up and poked my forehead with a finger. "Sorry ass nigga. What, you man enough to fuck me, but you ain't man enough to take care of your responsibilities once you get me pregnant? Now you talking 'bout going down to the clinic so you can kill our child... Scooby, you gotta be out of your mind. I would never kill no child that God blessed me with." By this time, I was standing up. "Ooh, I hate you." She pushed me. "And all this time I thought you actually cared about me. You buying me all this stuff. Taking care of my children. Spending all this time with us. Turns out you just as trifling as most niggas that's tramping around this hood!" She slumped back down on the couch and covered her face with her hands, tears were running down her forearms. "Then I'm finna lose my baby daddy. Marshall ain't gon' want nothing to do with me once he find out I'm pregnant with another man's baby. What am I gon' do?" She covered her face again, shaking her head.

The movers continued to remove the pieces of furniture that were around us until everything was gone except the couch that Amanda was crying on. I was so lost for words that it had affected my actions. I didn't know what I was supposed to say to this girl. I knew that her having that child would be a huge mistake. First off, I was damn near fifty. Secondly, she had a man that cared about her and her boys, and the truth was that I cared about her, but not enough to raise a family with her and three kids. No, suh. I wasn't prepared for that, and I wasn't even about to fake like I was. But on the other hand, if she was against abortion, then I would support her the best way that I knew how, and the best way I knew how to support anybody, including myself, was the streets. I hadn't changed in forty-eight years of living, and I never would.

I slid on the couch beside her and attempted to place my right arm around her.

As soon as she felt it, she jerked up. "Get off of me! Don't think that you can just throw your arm around me and everything is going to be all good. Scooby, you that damn grown, and you don't even know how to stand up and be a man. Damn, niggas just don't get it!" She started to pace, softly mumbling words to herself that I couldn't understand.

When I stood up, the movers grabbed the couch and took it on out the house, leaving us standing in an empty living room. The window was open, allowing a cool breeze to roam through the house. I was trying to stop smoking, but in that moment, I craved a Newport. I popped one in my mouth and lit it.

In mid pace, Amanda stopped, turning toward me. "Scooby, you know what? I'm the dumb one in this situation. I should have kept my legs closed. Any time a woman open her legs, a man gon' put something between them. You ain't wrong for fucking me. I'm the one that's wrong for allowing you to invade my temple. One thing you betta know is that I'm having this baby. I'm not gon' kill one of God's blessings to myself. All I ask is that you help me when I need assistance. You see how I'm struggling. You know what I go through on a daily basis. All the things you have done this far have been commendable, and I appreciate them. Just be there for me and our child. That's all I ask." She turned to walk away. I reached out and grabbed her arm, and she snatched it back. "Don't touch me! When I'm ready to talk to you again, I'll call you. Bye, Scooby."

I watched her walk out the front door with her head hung low. I knew I should have chased behind her, but I didn't have nothing to say that would make things any better. I wasn't ready to raise another child. And I already knew that her having this kid would cause me a lot of drama. But if I had known how much drama that was set to come my way over Amanda and that kid, I would've never messed with her in the first place.

* * *

Four months after I'd moved into my place, I got a call from Amanda that would change my life. After the big argument and her pregnancy revelation, we'd gotten back cool, and was sexing again like crazy. She was at my apartment more than I was, and occasionally I made trips over to her place. It was decided that we would have the baby, and that I would financially help her support the child. She would raise her with Marshall as the father. I was okay with that, and apparently, so was he. I didn't really know because I never spoke with him about the situation.

So, here it was four months later, in the depth of winter. Chicago was experiencing blizzard-like conditions. The wind and snow was so bad that if you held a hand up in front of your face you would not be able to see it. On top of that, it was freezing.

I'd confined myself to the house where I had the Isley Brothers' *Groove with You* playing in the background, and a fine thirty-five year old tenderoni on the couch, tooting up a line of pure Columbian cocaine. She was damn near naked, all but her panties and bra, laid on the arm of the sofa. High yellow, green eyes, and the body of a violin; she was a fox! And I was planning on digging deep into her foxhole.

She tooted her third line hard. Wiping her nose, she took a long sip from the glass of Korbel. "Say, daddy, you gon' come over here and play with me, or you gon' keep two-stepping to the Isley's. I promise stepping with me will be more fun." She smiled devilishly, opening her thick thighs, running her tongue across her lips.

I felt my nature rise. I was on my way to the couch when my cellphone rang. I cursed out loud and picked it up from the table next to the lamp. It was Amanda's number. "Yo, what's up, girl, you craving again? I asked. I'd driven over to her house so many times in the middle of the night for her cravings. She ate pickles and mustard on everything, even ice cream. Every time I went over there, we would up sexing.

"Scooby." Her voice was dry and raspy. "Scooby, Rallo just raped me."

Chapter 8
Binkey

Getting used to being in the county jail wasn't that hard. After a while, I simply adapted. I whooped three broads' asses over trying me because I'm small. After that, them hoes didn't mess with me no more. Majority of the females were plugged in gangs, but I had so much going on that my irritation was at an all-time high, when this one bitch became my first example. We were coming back from the gym, me rushing so that I could get to the shower before the other girls came and used up all the hot water.

The showers held ten women at a time. It was an open space with a pole that had ten shower heads on it going around in a circle. By the time I got into the shower I was number two, and was showering away when I noticed I had forgotten my shampoo. I had the conditioner, just not the shampoo. It was left on the bench in front of the shower. So, I dipped out for no less than ten seconds to grab it, when I turned back to my shower head, and there was this bull dyke in my shower, laughing and mugging me like everything was kosher.

I sucked my teeth. My heart began to race because I knew I was going to have to show this bitch what was good. I walked right back into the shower where she was. "Uh, excuse me, but this is my shower. I just went to get my shampoo."

She grunted, allowing the water to beat on her face before filling her mouth with it and spitting on my toes. "You move, you lose." She bellowed, giving me an intimidating stare.

I thought this bitch was nuts. This nasty, obese, monster of a tramp had just spat that nasty ass water out her mouth and onto my foot. I know she didn't. I nodded. "Okay."

I went over to the sink and poured out half of my shampoo, filled the rest with water, and shook it up. I looked over to the bull dyke and saw she was talking away with her back turned to me. I finished with what I was doing, and naked, slipped into the shower and tapped her on her back. When she turned around, I squirted the soap deep within her eyes, turned to my side and elbowed her square in the face while she screamed, reaching out trying to grab me, but she was blinded. I hit her with another elbow straight on, then put her in a headlock and crashed the top of her head into the shower wall. By this time, the other females had cleared the shower and watched the show. After her head crashed into the wall, she passed out; her body went limp. I straddled her and pummeled her face with blow after blow. Her blood pooled down the drain with the rest of the shower water. Once I knew that she was out cold, I kicked her to the side and finished my shower. The other girls watched me with their eyes bugged. I didn't pay them any attention.

The next day, the bull dyke got sent up to Dwight Corrections. She'd been awaiting transfer. She was sentenced to 75 years in prison for killing her lover and the man she caught her cheating with. She said that she'd catch me on the rebound. I wasn't worried.

The second event happened two months after the first. I'd returned early from rec one day, only to find my cellmate pleasuring herself to Heaven's son, who was essentially my nephew. She was an older woman of about 38. I flew into the room and snatched the picture from her hand. It was Tarig Junior at one of his swim meets. I turned to her with a disgusted look on my face.

She started to explain herself immediately. "Look, sista, I'm sorry. It's been a long time. I saw naked skin. Before I knew it, I—"

I had already blacked out. I slammed our cell door, flashed back to her and kicked her straight in the face. "Sick ass bitch!"

The sista had some fight in her. Even though blood spurted everywhere, she still tackled me with a piercing scream. I fell against the bars with her arms tightly around my waist. I could hear her breathing hard, still apologizing.

"Bitch, let me go! Come on! You woman enough to finger yourself off to some little kid, bitch. You should be woman enough to fight me head up, so let me go!" I was eager to get at her ass. Tarig Junior was my heart, and this bitch had the nerve to be violating his image. I wanted her ass bad.

She still wasn't trying to let me go. When I felt her teeth biting into my thigh, I lost it. I jerked my knee up with all my might and caught her square in the chin. She let me go and I caught her with another knee, then two lefts, then a right. Then, I blanked out while punching her life away. Before I knew it, blood was all over my face and the guards were struggling to get our cell open. When they finally did, they yanked me out. I kicked her in the face one more time before they drug me to the isolation room, which was their form of the hole. I didn't notice what I had done until about five minutes after they locked me in. I noticed they had stripped me of my clothes, and the freezing atmosphere perked my nipples. I had no bed, no blankets, just a metal toilet. I was sick.

"Y'all betta bring me some damn clothe. This shit ain't lawful." I felt tears coming down my eyes. "CO! Y'all betta bring me something to cover up with. You perverted muthafuckas! CO!" I started to shake the white bars, refusing to accept that this was my reality.

"Say sista, calm down. They gon' bring you clothes and bedding to you at midnight." I heard a distant voice say. It sounded muffled, almost alien-like.

"Who is that?" I looked around trying to locate where the woman could have possibly been.

"You see that vent that's over the toilet?"

I looked behind me and sure enough, there it was.

"That's where my voice is coming from. Our vents are connected. I am directly below you in a cell just like yours. My name is Earth."

Earth? What kind of name was that? I wanted to ask her but at the same time, I didn't want to be disrespectful.

"Have you been down here for a long time?" I really didn't care, but I was curious to find out if they kept people in this situation for long periods of time. I remembered Heaven telling me that Tarig was in the hole for 6 months straight before. I didn't think I was that strong to be able to sit in this cell for 6 months. Even the thought of it was getting me nervous and making me respect Tarig all at the same time.

"Naw, I been down here for only two months."

"Two months!" I gasped. I thought that I was going to pass out. I wanted to sit down, but I wasn't about to sit my naked ass on no cold metal. I just crouched down because I felt my legs getting weak. "What did you do to get put down here?" I prayed she had done something way worse than me. I was beginning to panic.

"Girl, all I did was call the CO a bitch, and I been down here ever since."

I rushed to the toilet and threw up. I dry heaved and threw up again and again until my stomach was empty. I flushed the toilet and gargled some water. I heard laughter coming through the vent. I couldn't understand what was so funny.

"Sista, what did you say your name was?" She asked. "Sista, what are you down here for?"

I didn't know her like that, but if she had been down there for two months, I figured I'd be down a lot longer so I might as well get to know her. She had to be a strong woman too because she spoke with an air that said she didn't have any worries.

"I'm Binkey and I'm down here for fighting. I just beat the blood out of my cellmate because she was pleasing herself to my 13-year-old nephew's picture." I said, standing on my tiptoes and talking with my face in the vent.

"How bad did you do her?" Her voice echoed. It sounded like she was talking through a tunnel, or Darth Vader's mask.

I thought about how she looked at final glance with blood coming from her nose and mouth. Her eyes were swollen. My silence must have said it all because I heard Earth laughing.

"Damn, that bad huh?" I heard her cough and what sounded like slaps to her chest. Then I heard the pipe churning downstairs, and the toilet flushing. I knew that most people flushed the toilet while they were running the water because it turned the water colder. The pipe continued to churn before it stopped abruptly. She cleared her throat. "Girl. I'm sorry, I damn near choked to death." She giggled and let out another cough. "You gone be straight Binkey, you shouldn't be down here more than ten days."

My mood perked up. "How you know that?" I prayed she was serious because I couldn't imagine staying in this cell for no two months. It was so small that I could touch both walls at the same time. I felt like I was in a sardine can. Worst of all, I was still naked. I felt violated. Tears started to run down my cheeks again, and bile started to rise within the pit of my stomach. Suddenly, I was missing my son. I was also missing Roman. I wondered if he still thought about me throughout the day. His last two letters had me deeply disturbed.

"Sista, I know that because like I said, I been down here two months and that's been the consensus. They don't keep people down here more than ten. That's usually the max." She coughed again, then cleared her throat. I heard her snort and spit into the toilet neglecting to flush. "They should bring you your clothes in a few hours. Right now, they got you on a control status. That means that your behavior is being monitored. This is their way of letting you know that you are not in control; they are. This is their first phase of the mental chastisement that you'll go through while you are down here. They gone start messing with your food, turning the air conditioning up to freeze you in that already cold cell up there. Your mail will also be delayed. You cannot allow this to break down your psyche. Being in this position will allow you to know just how strong you are." She started coughing again, then hocked what sounded like a lougie in the toilet. This time she flushed it though.

"Earth, why have you been down here so long if they only kept most down here for ten days?" I crossed my arms, rubbing my shoulders. I started dancing from one foot to the next trying to stay warm. My toes were starting to freeze up.

She laughed. "Aww me, I'm a special case. I'm what you call an A.C inmate. I'm on administrative confinement because I stabbed up two white devils that tried to jump me the last time I was here. Right now, I'm back in the county for court from that incident. I've already been sentenced to life for a murder rap I was found guilty of earlier this year. It was during that trial, they had me housed on the same unit you just came from. Them devils had the nerve to try and take my commissary because at the time the unit was dominated by the Aryan sisterhood. They wasn't even supposed to put me on that pod. Long story short, they tried me, and they struck out. I killed both of them, and would do it again if I could. The best feeling was looking back over my shoulder seeing their tongues hung out, dead."

There was a long silence between the both of us. I was blown away. I didn't know what to say next. She killed the silence again by laughing. "Girl, it's okay, things happen. If I wouldn't have gotten them, they would have gotten me. I made peace with the decisions I made a long time ago." She hocked, and I heard her spit in the toilet again. "This damn throat cancer is fucking me up. I can't wait until this suffering is over."

I swallowed hard. I continued to dance from one foot to the next. "When is your next court date?" I can't say that I honestly cared, but I wanted to keep the conversation going so that it would take my mind off of the cold.

"Three months from now."

"Three months! And they expect you to stay down here in this hole the whole time?" I couldn't believe what I was hearing. Now I started to worry about my own situation. What if my old cell mate did fall into a coma or what if something was seriously wrong with her. Would they charge me? I was already fighting a double murder, the last thing I needed was a third. Especially since my lawyer said things were looking up. I didn't regret what I had done to that sick broad. I just didn't want to face the possible consequences.

"Sista, one thing these people should never be allowed to have possession of is your mind. Physically, I belong to them, but mentally I control my own destiny. You see, they put me down here, isolated, because I changed over two of their precious skins. But every single month, right there in that cell block you just came from, at least one sista gets killed. As long as it's black on black, or white killing black, or Spanish killing black, the most you gone get back here is ten days, and maybe a case. They treat me so rough because this is my third white killing." Her coughing started again, and I heard her slapping her chest, and spitting. No flush. "Sista, I hate everything about them devils. I been in foster care my whole life and I haven't ever been to one where I was not molested or beaten by a white predator."

Just then a guard came and ran his night stick across my bars. He stopped and ogled my naked body, licking his lips. He grabbed his crotch, then snapped out of it when a female C.O. showed up.

"Get out of here you damn pervert!" The heavy set black woman said. She was shorter than me and looked to weigh about three hundred pounds. Her hair was whipped though, and she had rings on every finger. She even had the nerve to be wearing some Retro all black Jordan #3's. In her arms were two blankets, two sheets, a pillowcase and an orange prison jump suit. "Open B-40!" She yelled to the control desk. My cell popped with a loud click. She handed me everything, including my orange shoes that looked like they belonged to a karate fighter. I didn't care how they looked, as long as they was able to keep my feet warm. "Here you go Miss." She closed the cell and stared at me while I got dressed. I started to feel uneasy. "What made you kick that woman ass the way you did? She had to be taken to the hospital and everything."

I was finally dressed. I felt the anger coursing through me all over again. I didn't know what business it was of hers, but at that point I really didn't care. I was mad. "I caught that bitch two fingers deep in her pussy, while looking at my 13-year-old nephew's picture."

She nodded in understanding.

"Still, a lil' bitty thang like you don't look like she could inflict so much damage. That girl is fucked up. You shouldn't be surprised if they try to charge you over that. They gone want somebody to pay for her hospital bills and you already should know how cheap the city of Chicago is." She sighed, looking me up and down. "Alright then, my name is Miss Jackson. Call me if you need anything. I work 2nd and 3rd shift but mostly 3rd. You smoke?"

I scrunched up my face.

"Smoke what?"

I was curious, and hoping she was talking about some green. Man, if I had me some Mary Jane, I would be able to do this hole stuff with no problem. I walked closer to the gate.

"Girl, are you crazy? You should know that all I'm talking about is a few Newports." She looked from her left to right.

I smiled. "Naw, no thanks. I never did take up that habit, but I really do appreciate it though." I couldn't hide the disappointment from my voice.

"Alright then. I'll do occasional rounds to check on you to make sure you alright. You ain't suicidal or nothing, are you?" She gave me a bewildered look.

"No." I crossed my arms, looking at her like she had seriously lost her mind.

"Good, I ain't think so. You look like one of them strong young sistas. Proud! Listen to Earth, that sista is deep. Hold ya head and let me know if that pervert come sniffing around you."

After she left, me and Earth stayed up all night shooting the shit. She had so many stories, and had been through so much that it was like I was listening to one movie after the next. We wound up kicking it every single day through the vent for hours and hours on end. Before I knew it ten days had flown by. I still had not heard anything from the County Jail Hearing Committee. I had received my writeup for the battery on the 7th day, so I didn't know what was going on, and then I found out one early morning on my 13th day of being down there.

The C.O. woke me up, didn't allow me to properly brush my teeth before he carried me away in handcuffs and sat me down in front of the ugliest black man I have ever seen in a suit. He had to be about six feet four inches tall, and every bit of two hundred and sixty pounds. He looked like an obese version of Flava Flav, except for he was balding.

He read me my Miranda Rights immediately. "You have the right to remain silent. Anything you say, can and will be used against you in the court of law. You have the right to an Attorney. If you cannot afford an Attorney, one will be provided for you. Do you understand your rights?" He asked without looking up from the file on his desk.

"Yeah, I do."

"And would you still like to proceed with this interview?

"Yes, what is this about?" I felt my stomach flipping over.

He sat a tape recorder on the table and pressed the record button.

"This interview is being conducted because you are suspected of Battery by Prisoner on the above date and—"

"I want a lawyer."

The C.O. came, got me, threw me into my cell, and slammed the bars. I ran to my vent and screamed Earth's name until she woke up, and told her everything.

"Binkey, it's just Battery. You probably gone get some probation for that, don't worry. Your main concern should be them murders you were telling me they was trying to charge you with."

That same day I heard my writeup in front of the hearing committee, and they gave me two more days to serve in Isolation. I wasn't tripping. 48 hours would be nothing for me, especially since I had Earth downstairs.

Out the blue that night, Earth blindsided me. "Sista, what is your religion? Who do you believe in?"

"Girl, I believe in Jesus. Who else am I supposed to believe in?" Though I wasn't the most religious person in the world, I did believe in God. "Why, who do you believe in?" I whispered curious.

"I believe in the God that made Jesus. I believe in the God that Jesus bowed down on his knees and prayed too five times a day. The God, that they say looked to the Heavens to while he was being crucified, and asked, why have you forsaken me?"

"Oh." I was still curious. "What is your God's name?"

"There is only one God, sista and he has 99 names, but the most sacred is Allah, the one true God. It is this Deity, that Jesus tasted for and prayed too. It is the God of those before Jesus. The God of Abraham, Noah, Moses, David, Solomon and so many other prophets, including Jesus and Muhammad. May Allah's peace and blessings be upon them all.

She spent the next four hours blowing my mind and answering every question that I had. The more she spoke, the clearer I saw things. Her delivery was poetic and natural. Before I went to bed that night, I found myself questioning my beliefs. The next day was more of the same. She spent twelve hours in the vent giving it to me in a row. Explaining how our people had been stripped of our culture and of our root religion of Islam. She took me back and through the struggles of the Moors who crossed over to Africa, then the United States and broke down the Garvey movement and its importance. Then, she broke down the concept behind The Moorish Science Temple of America, which she was blessed in. The movement of Noble Drew Ali brought tears to my eyes, especially since my mother's parents were Moroccan, and had navigated from North Africa. I was seeing things in a new light, so much so that I refused to leave my cell the first time they came. They threatened that I would have to do another month if I didn't follow the direct order to return to General Population. I walked to my cell door and slammed it. The guard walked off, shaking his head.

Over the next four weeks, Earth would take me on mystical mental journeys that put me in tune with my culture and our history. She sent me books, and pamphlets, research tools, and I studied everything over and over again. It was like a drug that I couldn't get enough. By the time it came for me to get out again, I was ready to refuse when Earth said. "Sista, it's okay. Continue your studies and fight for your case. Use the knowledge in which Allah has instilled in you. You are a jewel. Your purpose is far greater than you understand right now but in due time you will.

Your purpose is far greater than you understand right now but in time Allah will reveal his treasures to you. Be steadfast and pursue your new identity from the Temple. You are not Binkey, you are a powerful black Muslim woman that has to find her Iman. I pray that Allah blesses you and guides your every endeavor. I love you sista, and I leave you in peace. As-salam-Alaikum."

Tears were pouring down my cheeks by this point. "Uva-Laikum-Asalam."

They moved me to the same cell block. When I came through the door with my bedding, all eyes were on me. Women whispered to each other as I passed, while others got out of my way. They moved me upstairs to a cell with a sister that had long dreadlocks. The first thing I saw when I entered the cell was her Quran. I smiled and looked toward the heavens because that had to be a sign. She was writing a letter at the desk and looked up as she saw me.

"Oh, I'm sorry. Let me get out your way while you move in."

All of her stuff was on the bottom bunk, so I took the top. The room smelled of Somali Rose. I saw what must have been her prayer rug folded across her bed. She was stepping out of the room when I asked.

"Sista, are you Muslim?" That must have caught

her off guard because her face looked distorted.

She turned around, ready for confrontation. "Yeah, is that going to be a problem? They just moved a girl out of here because she couldn't respect me and give me my space when I needed to pray. I don't got nothing against nobody else's religion. I just winna be left alone to praise Allah." She said pointing to the sky.

I held my hands up. "Sista. As-salam-Alaikum."

"What's your name Sista?" She asked.

"Right now, I'm still working on that."

"Well my name is Khadijah`El, and we gone work on your re-birth, al-hamdulillah!"

Khadijah became my best friend, just like Earth. For the next couple months, we, along with ten other sistas would study the Deen and get deep. During this rebirth, I became Aishah. It seemed like as soon as I accepted Islam, everything began to fall in place.

Hood Rich

Chapter 9
Heaven

My stomach was full of butterflies. I was feeling sick. On top of that, my nerves were making my legs impossible to stand on. I took a deep breath. Come on girl, you can do this. This ain't the first time you been under these conditions. I needed to get a hold of myself. I shook out my arms, cracked my neck and kicked both feet looking like a damn fool to the people in line behind me. Finally, I stepped through the metal detector, was cleared and handed the woman at the desk my driver's license.

An older white woman with a scowl on her face took it, eyed the card, then me from the corner of her eyes. She shook her head and handed the card back to me.

"You gone be at table Seven and no standing for long periods of time. You get to have one physical embrace consisting of a hug or kiss, neither lasting long than sixty seconds. No singing, rapping, or smuggling illegal paraphernalia. She stopped, looked me up and down, then grunted. "Be respectful at all times and know that we are watching you closely."

I smiled sarcastically. I had been to this place more than a thousand times, and this broad knew that, yet she still went through the motions. I was more irritated than anything. I looked over my shoulder and saw she was going through the same routine with the next younger black sista who started questioning her.

"Lady, what I look like bringing something in here? What, you think everybody my color up to no good? Do you see my daughter with me? Do you think that I would risk her freedom for anybody?" She rolled her eyes. "Give me my I.D. so I can go see my daughter's father." She snatched the card back from the woman and picked her daughter up, mumbling to herself. The little girl looked like a little confused angel. They flew past me and sat down at their assigned table.

Let me quit being nosey. I shook my head, trying to snap out of the zone that being nosey had me in. I cashed in a twenty-dollar bill and got back all quarters. After stopping at the vending machines, I secured a double cheeseburger, barbeque wings, two bags of Flaming Hots, M&M's, and a grape pop. All of Tarig's favorite snacks. I sat everything down on the table and eyed the door that Tarig usually came through.

The visiting room was unusually packed. Some of every race was jammed into the small 41-tabled area. Some women dressed up, some didn't. Kids ran around screaming, chasing one another. One little boy had a booger on his finger chasing what had to be his sister while she screamed at the top of her lungs while her blonde mother yelled for them to sit down and shut up.

I must have been waiting for 40 minutes. Finally, I got irritated and went to the officer's desk. As soon as he saw me, his pink face frowned as if he was irritated. I didn't care, I was used to the ill treatment.

"Excuse me officer." I paused, glancing at his name tag. "Maxwell, I've been here nearly an hour. Can you please tell me what is taking so long?" Before he could even respond I saw Tarig come through the door with a full beard but looking as good as I have ever seen him. His eyes were searching around the visiting room, probably looking for Tarig Junior who always ran to him.

"Thanks anyway, officer." I turned and walked swiftly to my man. "Hey baby, oh my God I missed you so much."

He turned, saw me and lifted me up in the air before kissing all over my lips and playing "Tongue smackdown". No matter what, Tarig always got my juices flowing just by kissing me and holding me to his body. After all these years, I was still hooked.

Our kiss ended with both of us groaning. He held my hand as we sat down. I'd never saw him with a full beard before. He looked distinguished, and even more handsome. There was just nothing he could do that would not make desire him. "Baby, I never seen you with a beard before." I whined.

He smiled. "I been in that hole for the last 6 months. I haven't had time to shave. I was getting my hair cut when they called me out the blue."

"Babe, as soon as I found out you was getting out the hole today, I took off work early and made my way up here. I been missing you so damn much." I lifted his hand and kissed it. "How are your books? Do you need any money or for me to order you anything from the catalogs?"

"Maybe later boo, I'll send you a letter once I go over everything!" He looked concerned. Worry lines appeared across his forehead. "Where is my son?"

I bit the side of my lip. I didn't want to tell him that Champ had took Tarig Junior on a shopping spree along with his lil girlfriend to New York. He promised Tarig Junior that if he got a 3.5 G.P.A or better on his report card that he would take him out east on a spree and he could bring anyone that he wanted. Of course, he chose Elizabeth, his girlfriend, and of course I was jealous.

"Baby, Tarig Junior having girl problems. Well not problems. Let's just say that some girl got his nose wide open. He is spending time with her. He earned it. He got a 3.5 G.P.A last semester.

Tarig started laughing. "You mean he is spending time with that green eyed, half breed, girl he sent me pictures of?" He slapped his thighs, cutting up, acting like he had heard the funniest joke in the world. "That's my baby. She cute too. He got that taste like his Pops."

I blushed. "Is that supposed to be a compliment?" I asked, batting my eye lashes.

"Aww, naw ma'. She way prettier than you was when you were her age. I wish I had got that lucky." He teased, avoiding looking at me as I smacked his thigh and pinched him. He laughed again with his beard moving up and down on his face. It was the first time I'd noticed how much weight he'd lost.

"Babe, are you losing weight?" I was concerned.

"He pulled his shirt up rubbing his hand across a perfect eight pack. His stomach was sorta hairy, but you could still make out the muscles underneath it clearly. "Yeah ma', they been starving me."

I got up. "Well, let me go heat this food up."

I sat back and watched him eat and gave him a brief update of what was going on. I told him how Seven had made it to the elite 8, but they were put out by a Cinderella team from California. I told him how Brittany had just gotten her Bachelor's degree, and that Seven was even talking marriage. I skated around giving him the 411 on Roman because I didn't want him to worry. So, I just gave him some simple info. What he said next blew my mind.

"I heard you been fucking with one of his partners." He said this while chewing, and washing down the food with the grape pop. He didn't look at me as he tilted his head back. I watched his Adams apple go up and down as he took strong swallows. All the sudden my nervousness was cutting in again. I just knew the visit was going too smoothly.

"Tarig, do you really want to do this? Can't we just enjoy this visit? I ain't seen you in damn near seven months."

He curled up his lip with a look of disgust written across his face. "That's the hardest part about being in prison. Knowing that eventually you have gotta give up some pussy. Some nigga gotta fuck my woman. I know it's all a part of the game, but that shit still sucks, Heaven." He clenched his jaw. "What this nigga's name?" He was now looking at me for the first time.

I was biting my freshly manicured nails. This man still had that effect on me. I began to fidget in my seat. It felt like they had turned the heat up in the visiting room. "His name is Charles." I stuttered.

He grunted. "Charles, huh? Where you meet him at?"

"Does that matter?" I whispered.

His eyebrows closed in on his forehead. "Yeah it matter! Have this dude been around my son?" He moved the food from in front of him, looking as if he was ready to jump across the table.

"Tarig, calm down right now. You getting me real nervous." He had never hit me before, but the look on his face told me that he was ready to blow. I already knew he was crazy about his son.

"Yes, Tarig, he's been around him, but J.R know who his father is. He knows that I will never put another man before you or show affection toward that man while he is around. I just been kind of lonely." I said while looking at the floor, afraid to meet his eyes.

"Heaven, has this stud been in our house?" He lifted my chin. "In our bed, Goddess?" His voice was raspy. He kept swallowing trying to compose himself.

I was already crying real tears. I reached and grabbed his hand, while wiping my nose. I didn't care about the crazy stares everybody was giving me. I could see that Tarig was hurt.

"Damn!" He jerked his hand away. "I hate being in love with you while I'm in here, this shit ain't healthy for me." He was silent for a long time. "Sometimes you women break us brothers up in here more than this prison do." He rose. "Man, Heaven live your life. I can't take you breaking me down no more. Just make sure Tarig Junior stay in touch." He finished his pop and walked away, without looking back.

I sat at that table crying until the guard told me I had to leave.

Chapter 10
Roman

I was set to get on a plane to Miami at 9 PM. I had everything packed and ready to go. The reason for the trip was business. Moeshe needed a middleweight Heroin player knocked off so that he could control the flow coming from out East. The hit would bring me seventy- five thousand dollars and a showroom Benz that was set to come out next year.

Since becoming Champ's marksman, I'd been to Arizona, Cali, Georgia, Wisconsin, and now Miami bussing moves. The kills helped me to forget about Binkey for the moment. When I felt like breaking down and crying, I often went to Champ craving a job and he always had one lined up, and I was always paid up front.

I took a deep breath and checked into the Cook County Jail with my son closely bundled in my arms. I hadn't seen Binky in months. Today was the day for her and Heaven to usually visit, but my sister advised me that I should go. So, I sat on the other side of the glass holding my son waiting for her to walk in.

When she did, I felt my eyes water. She was getting so slim. Her hair was now in the beginning process of dreads. She had no make-up on, and around her neck was a star and crescent moon. Her eyes bugged out when she saw me. She turned to look at our son, tears began to flow from her eyes while we both picked up the phone at the same time. I spoke first.

"Hey baby, you are looking so skinny."

She nodded, tears still flowing. "I know, wait..."

She cleared her throat. "As-salami-Altium Wa Rahmatullani Baracatuh."

Now it was time for me to bug my eyes out. I returned her greeting. "Wa Alaikum As Salamu Wa Rahmatullani Wa Baracatuh." I smiled. "Baby, you a Muslim now?" I was ecstatic.

"I'm a Moor. I believe in the Science of Islam. But yes, I submit my will to the one true God, Allah." She pointed upward. "How have you been?"

I didn't know where to begin. I told her everything within a five-minute segment. The whole time I held Jaheim up to the glass so she could look him over. He kept smacking the glass with both of his hands, drool running down to his shirt with both dimples showing.

She smiled while listening, making faces at him. I saw the hurt on her face, but she tried to be strong. She tried to put on a brave front. I knew her, I knew better.

"Roman, I'm so worried about you. You and him are all I been thinking about baby. I need for you to be out there when I get there. I don't want you to be coming in here while I'm on my way out. My lawyer said that I got a 90 percent chance of beating this. They ain't really got nothing other than that machete and I could have purchased that anywhere." She started to bite her nails, a nervous trait she'd picked up from Heaven. "Roman, I don't want to live without you no more."

Those words kept replaying themselves over and over again in my head as I slung my suitcase on the bed at what had to be one of the sleaziest hotels in Miami. Though it was freezing in Chicago, in Miami it was in the mid 70's, and slightly humid. People were walking around in shorts and white beaters like it was the middle of the summer. Most of the women I saw wore tight biker shorts, with half t-shirts. I couldn't believe how many beautiful women there was in one place at one time. That was the scene that greeted me when I left that airport.

Outside of the Sweet Dreams motel I'd checked into, were prostitutes looking for a trick. The majority of them had on cheap furs that hung open showcasing their bikini clad treasures. As I walked to my room door, they accosted me.

"Say honey, look like you all alone. You need some company?" A dark skinned sista said with her coat open. She licked her lips and ran her fingers along the waistband of her satin red panties. "I promise not to bite, less you want me too." She added seductively.

"Tina, he look like he can afford both of us." Her caramel friend said kissing Tina on the cheek, then squeezing her own boobs. I looked them both up and down. They looked country thick. Had I not been on business, I would have definitely tested the waters, but I had to remain focused.

Just then, a Benz pulled up. It was all white with black tinted windows. I saw the driver's window roll down, and an arm flailing wildly. The man was barking orders. He had to be their pimp because they looked scared for their lives. I watched them jog then stop abruptly, strutting sexily on the busy street he'd directed them too. Before his window rolled up, we made eye contact. A dark-skinned face with a mouth full of gold. He looked me up and down. Being no more than twenty feet away from me, I could hear the Schoolboy Q coming out of his system. He nodded. "Whud up?"

I nodded back, turning the key into my door.

"Say homie, before you leave you should let my girls straighten you out. They got the best pussy around Florida, Grade A certified." He put a cigarillo to his lips and pulled, making the cherry light up.

"I'll keep that in mind." I said opening the door.

"Yeah, you make sure you do that. I'll make sure they take care of you real nice." He looked me up and down before his window slowly concealed his face, putting him behind tint.

I stepped into the door. There was a king-sized bed in the middle of the room, which a big cockroach was slowly crawling across. It had an egg coming out of its behind. The blanket looked worn and overused. The carpet had more stains on it than a smoker's teeth. There was a small table next to the bed with a lamp and a King James Version Bible. The air smelled stale, the light was flashing off and on, threatening to go out. In the two minutes I had been in there, I had seen not one, but two rats run across the floor. I simply shrugged. I wasn't a stranger to the conditions. If it was one thing residents of Chicago were used too, it was rats and roaches.

I flung my bag on top of the bed, killing the roach in the process. I checked over the contents making sure everything had made it along with me. The most important things were my false identifications. Without them, the job couldn't be pulled off.

I pulled out the Mark's picture. Sazo'n , a Brazilian muscle that was slowly moving up the ladder after his brother had gotten killed eighteen months ago. He had family ties all over the Midwest. Since his brother's murder, he'd began to deal heavily with the three cities, Chicago, Cleveland and Gary. These were some of the most profitable cities when it comes to dealing heroin. Sazo'n was much more established in these parts because of his family's ties. Champ had said that once he was knocked off, it would open up a whole window for cash flow. I figured that had to be the case if he was putting up 75 thousand dollars.

Me personally, I didn't care who Saz'on was or what kind of family ties he had. My main concern was that within the next day or so, he would be changed over. I had a job to do and against all odds, it would get done.

My cell rang at 9:30pm that night. It was Champ telling me that everything had been situated, and that I could go pick up the car that was waiting for me at the airport. I told him that I would see him in few days. We hung up.

I'd been standing since I got in the room, not really wanting to touch none of the line. I was fearing the absolute worst that could come from doing that. I decided that even though I was somewhat tired, I would go and get the whip Champ had sent.

I called a cab and it pulled up an hour later. I never saw an Asian drive a cab before that night. He demanded I pay him up front by banging on the partition with a .38 special.

"Hey, you, 2Pac, you pay right now. No wait till later, you pay up front." The whole time he talked he waved the gun around as if it was the most normal thing in the world to be doing.

Instead of getting pissed off, I couldn't help but to laugh. To me it looked like his eyes were all the way closed. I didn't feel threatened or disrespected. I slid him a twenty. "Take me to the airport." I said, closing the door and watching him as he adjusted his rear-view mirror to see my clearer.

"You from somewhere else, not here, are you?" He asked making a U-turn to get back out of the parking lot. He had to be about sixty years old. His face was round, hair receding, which made his face look like it was melting. I still couldn't get over the fact that he talked with his eyes closed. That was funny to me.

I smirked. "Nah, kid, I'm from New York." I lied. I didn't want to get into no long drown out conversation with him. For all I knew he could have been the Feds.

"Yeah, I taught' so, looka like you from up ta're."

No more words were exchanged.

I found the whip Champ described to me in the same parking spot he said it would be in. A black on black STS Cadillac with tint windows. I stuck my hand under the front bumper and felt until the key fell in my hand. I opened the door and slid into the peanut butter leather seats. The car smelled brand new. He'd told me that it was fresh off the lot, and that if I wanted it afterward, I could keep it. I reached under the seat on the passenger side and located a black box. I sat it on my lap land opened it with a loud click.

Inside was a P250 Compact light and laser pistol. I took it out looking it over. All black with the egg like scope on top of it. I aimed it downward and tapped the trigger softly. A green beam appeared from the egg. In the box were two clips and a silencer. I couldn't help smiling. I bit my bottom lip and nodded.

Back at the motel, I recovered a 715T flat top with a Red Dot 9 millimeter LR, and a MP-15 sport rifle with a scope. It was one of the prettiest semi-automatic rifles I had ever seen. I was geeked and ready for whatever. There was also a case of hunter's knives that had me salivating. I didn't know too much about Sazo`n, but what I did know was that his ass was out.

Hood Rich

Chapter 11
Heaven

When I got back home, I sat on my bed crying for two hours. I cried until I couldn't manage anymore tears. I couldn't believe that Tarig was walking out of my life. I couldn't believe that after all we had been through that this was our final chapter. I felt sick. My phone rang. It was Charles telling me that he was on his way home. I almost told him not to come, but he hung up the phone before I could get my words out. I didn't know if I wanted to see him again. I felt so terrible and weak. I had no energy to fight. It had been the first time in a long time that I actually felt like giving up on life.

"Momma?" Tarig Junior knocked on my bedroom door before opening it, catching me wiping tears from my eyes as he walked in, I tried to give him a weak smile, though I couldn't help sniffling.

"What's up babe?" I managed. He was looking more and more like his father every single day. I'd noticed two days ago the peach fuzz developing on his upper lip. He even had a few whiskers growing on his chin. I couldn't believe my son was becoming a man right before my eyes. Pretty soon, he'd be leaving me too. I swallowed hard, fighting back tears.

He came in, sitting on the bed next to me, placing his right arm around my shoulders. "What's the matter momma? I heard you crying all the way in the living room." His voice was starting to scratch, switching from being that of a child to that of a man. I could feel the muscle wrapped around my shoulder.

He was really growing up.

"Baby I'm okay, I'm just going through something right now. It'll pass." I reassured him, trying once again to hold back tears and failed as they began to cascade down my cheeks. I was trying my best to be strong in front of him, but I couldn't help imagining him also walking out my life in less than 5 years when he turned 18. I would be all alone. What would I do? What would my purpose be?

He got up and stood in front of me kissing me on the forehead. "Tell me what's going on. You're supposed to be my best friend, and best friends don't hold secrets from each other. So, what's going on, Queen?" He tilted my head upward by touching my chin.

I don't know why I did it, but I told him everything. The whole conversation between me and his father. I didn't leave one word out that we had shared on that visit. By the time I was done talking, tears were all over my face and he was holding me to his chest and rubbing my back.

After twenty minutes of this, he directed me to look at him. "Momma, Pops, just going through something right now. You already know how jealous he is over you. Then you told him that this dude been in his house, and around me. Then, I didn't help matters any by not coming to visit him with you. You can't think that this is the end of y'all. Trust me it isn't. We gone go visit him next Saturday, together, and talk about this like a family. You been holding him down for too long got him to simply call it quits just because he jealous of some dude that don't really matter to neither one of us. Unless, you love Charles or something." He lowered his voice. "Do you?"

I shook my head. The truth was that I cared about Charles, but I could never feel for no man what I felt for Tarig.

"Of course, not baby. I love your father." I pulled him to me and wrapped my arms around him, burying my head into his chest. "You gone go with me Saturday?" I asked looking up to him.

He nodded. "Of course, we're a family and ain't nothing gone break that apart." He kissed me on the forehead again, making me smile.

"Umm, Tarig, I gotta get home." Elizabeth said appearing in the doorway. She looked absolutely beautiful with her long hair pulled back into a ponytail. Her green eyes popped. She gave me a warm smile and waved. "Bye momma, see you tomorrow. Lord willing."

Tarig looked down at me. "You gone be okay, beautiful?"

I nodded. "Go ahead and see her out. I'll be okay." I assured him while waving goodbye to Elizabeth.

Tarig came through the visiting room door looking good as ever. Now he was freshly shaven, his waves were flicking, and his clothes looked crisped, along with the Timberlands boots I'd ordered him. He had me going through a thang from a distance. My stomach was doing flips, but that didn't distract me from yearning for him.

Tarig Junior walked over to him and wrapped his arms around him. He was getting taller, already standing up to his father's chin. They walked over to the table where I was seated. I didn't know whether to get up and give him a hug like I usually did, or stay seated. I was confused. I started biting my nails, forgetting about the fresh manicure.

He sat down without pressing the issue and that hurt me so bad. I wanted to cry. I didn't even meet his eyes. For the first ten seconds, everyone was silent.

"I can't believe that I'm the 13-year-old." Tarig Junior shook his head in disgust. "What, all the sudden you two are enemies? Y'all can't even hug or kiss?" Tears glazed his eyes.

I swallowed hard, still not knowing what to do, or say for that matter. I peeked over at Tarig. His head was bowed looking at the floor. He reached down and picked some lint off the top of his boots.

"I missed you Tarig," I said softly, looking at my hands. "I will always love you, no matter what you may think, and I will never put another man before you."

He wiped both palms on the legs of his pants, tilted his head back and took a deep breath.

"Damn, Heaven. Boo, you know my nose wide open for you. I ain't slept in days. I keep imagining you with some other man in or bed, and our son calling him daddy. You know how crazy I am over y'all, and how much family means to me. You know I would never give up on us. I just needed time to think. By the way, I just got approved for boot camp. I leave next Tuesday and six months from then I'm gone be home. A new law passed concerning the overcrowding in the Illinois prison system. Everybody under ten years getting boot camp now." He smiled.

I couldn't even breathe. I kept repeating six

months... over and over again in my mind, until I was saying it out loud. Now I was really choked up.

"Baby, you coming home in six months?" I can't believe it.

He nodded. "Six months, boo. Iesha` Allah."

Tarig Junior spoke up. "You see, God got a plan for this family."

I silently thanked God for this blessing. I wouldn't miss a Sunday of church until God brought my man home. All I had to do now was get rid of Charles. He had to go, money and all.

Hood Rich

Chapter 12
Scooby

I almost choked on my own spit. My cocaine high going away immediately. I ran my hand over my hair which I had slicked to the back with pomade and passed gas. My stomach was doing somersaults. I squeezed the phone so tight I heard the plastic cracking. "What do you mean he just raped you?" I growled.

I could hear her crying and sniveling. Her groaning echoed into the phone. Every time she tried to speak, she broke down again. I could also hear her children in the background crying.

"Scooby, I'm on my way to the hospital right now. I want you to meet me down there. I'm going to Christ Hospital out in Hyde Park. Please come, I really need you right now." She started to break down again before she hung up.

I was so mad that I was seeing stars. I knew damn well Rallo ain't pull no trick shit like that. I picked my phone back up and dialed his number. It rang and rang without him answering. I decided against leaving a voicemail, that was never my thang. Finally, I sent him a text to call me ASAP. I showed my lady friend the door, and I hit the blizzard on my way to Christ Hospital.

As soon as I got into the hospital, I went to the Emergency Room desk. A heavy-set woman with way too much make up acted like she didn't see me. She was too busy talking on the phone and looking at her ugly dark-skinned face in the mirror. She was plucking at her eyebrow, then flicking whatever was on her fingers. I waited until she had the nerve to open a Snickers bar before I slapped my hand on the desk.

"Hey! Get your ass off that phone and tell me where my baby mother is!" I glared at her with so much hatred I could tell she got scared.

She swallowed and finally put her snack down. Into the phone, she said, "Girl I'll call you back later." All the while looking at me from the corner of her eyes. She hung up. "Sorry about that, sir. Can you please tell me your lady's name?" She sounded so sweet and professional all the sudden.

"Her name is Amanda Stevens and she shouldn't have come in more than an hour ago." Due to the fact that it was practically a blizzard outside, the Emergency Room wasn't that crowded. I was glad I'd remembered Amanda's last name. I'd gotten her mail by accident more than once.

She drug her pudgy fingers down a clipboard, then flipped the page as if she had all day. "Aww, here we go. She's in room 307. I'll call the nurse upstairs and tell her you're coming." She waved me off.

I took the stairs two at a time. When I made it to the third floor, I was in a panic running up and down the hall looking at room numbers. When I found room 307, the door was closed. I turned the knob and barged in anyway. "Amanda—"

There was a woman between her legs with a white coat on. Amanda's feet were in stirrups. She was laid on her back with her children standing by her head, both crying.

The doctor shot up. "Excuse me! But you have to get out of here. This is a restricted area!" The small white woman yelled with her glasses moving up and down on her nose. She pointed toward the hallway. "Out now!"

"No Dr. Ralph, that's my child's father. I need him in here with me for moral support, please." Amanda begged.

The doctor thought about it for a moment. "Alright, but you have to stand over there." She pointed to the top of the bed where Amanda sat up halfway.

When I stood by her, she reached out to me and wrapped her arms around my neck. "Thank you for coming baby, it really means so much to me."

I nodded, crouched down and wrapped my arms around her two sons. I was surprised how they took to me. As soon as I hugged them, they stopped crying. I comforted them the best way that I could. I clenched my jaw the whole time disbelieving what my best friend had done.

After the doctor assured us the baby was okay, I felt a little bit better. Amanda only had a few nicks and bruises across her face, and wrists from where he held her down. She was interviewed by two detectives and she told them just enough to get them on their way. I had already told her that this wasn't a police matter, I was going to take care of this personally. So, she gave them a bogus description of him.

The more I stood there watching her explain what happened, I started to think about my own daughter who I hadn't seen in a while. I missed her a lot, her and her brother.

I even missed their mother who had recently

passed away. Seeing Amanda in that bed made me want to get in contact with my kids. I know I'd made a promise to their mother many years ago, but my heart was yearning for my kids.

Somehow, we wound up making it back to her place in one piece. The streets were so bad that the car did two three-sixties before we made it to her home safely. I fed the boys and she put them to bed. Neither of us ate much but I drank a beer, while she laid on my chest as we sat on the couch.

"Tell me what happened."

She took a deep breath. "He knocked on the front door. When I went to answer it, I asked who it was. He said his name and I told him you weren't here. At first, there was silence but then he stated that he needed to use the bathroom and asked if he could use mine. I hesitated, but wound up opening the door. I could smell the liquor on him immediately. He told me I looked beautiful as he walked past and headed upstairs." Her voice started to break up. "After he used the bathroom, he came out and said thank you. So, I assumed all was well. But then he spotted your coat that you'd left on my bed. He walked into my bedroom and picked it up. He asked why it was there and I told him you'd left it some days ago. He said that it was really his coat and that he'd been missing it for a few weeks. He started to leave out the room with it and I tried to grab it from him. He yanked it back laughing like it was all a big joke. Finally, I told him to let it go, and he did. I told him to leave my house and he started to but then he stopped mid stride and turned toward me. He asked what I saw in you? What did you have that he didn't? I asked him to ask you that before I told him to leave again. That's when the expression on his face changed. I got scared. I told him to leave again. He licked his lips then attacked me, tackling me to the bed and ripping my gown off. I screamed for him to stop, but he didn't. I told him that I was pregnant. That seemed to excite him. He slapped me across the face, yanking my panties off and ..."

By this time, she was breaking down with her face in her lap. Her hands covering it while tears dripped through her fingers. She rocked back and forth. And it was at that moment that I knew I was going to kill my best friend.

I got a text from him at two-thirty that next afternoon. I called him right away. He picked up after four rings.

"Main man, what it be like?"

"What it be like?" Say blood, where are you? We need to sit down and talk. Let's smoke somethin' I got a few crystals that gone lift you up!" I said looking over the weapons on my bed. I wanted to kill Rallo right then. I was hungry!

"Well, right now I'm with my Ivory mama and we shopping, I'll be back over toward the ghetto later on tonight. My brother having a spade game. Drop by there around eight. I'll be over there."

I wanted to tell his ass to meet me right then, but I ain't want to spook him. "Alright main man, I'll drop through later on, make sure you be there. Don't have me fucking around with your people and you ain't there."

He laughed. "Naw, cat daddy, fly-low baby, I will.... be there." He hung up.

My heart was pounding in my chest. I tasted the salt in my mouth, and I couldn't stop clenching my jaw. I fired a pebble to calm me down and let the high take over me. Rallo's clock was ticking.

When I pulled up at his brother's duplex four hours later, Rallo's car was parked out front. I slammed my car in park so hard that it jerked to a halt. I didn't even park all the way before I was on the porch and knocking on the door. After thirty seconds, his brother answered the door with no shirt on, scratching his fat hairy belly.

" What's up, Scooby?" He rasped, obviously coming out of a deep sleep. His breath smelled worse than sewage.

I brushed past him and into the house. The place was all but empty with the exception of Darryl's wife sitting on the couch watching the Real Housewives of Atlanta.

"Hey Scooby." She waved.

I nodded. "Where is Rallo?"

Darryl came in and closed the door. "Rallo went to Burger King to pick us some food up. Why? He questioned.

I ignored him. "The Burger King is on 65th. How he do that when his car is still outside?"

Darryl, continued to scratch his belly. "He used mine because his been acting up." He plopped down on the couch next to his wife.

Something wasn't adding up. "Ain't you having a spade game here tonight?"

He gave me a look like I had lost my mind. "Spade game, that ain't until next weekend, after I get my check."

Just then, my phone rang. "What's up?"

"Nigga, I been knowing you yo' whole life. You don't think I know when you out to get a nigga. Ever since you been fucking with that young bitch, we ain't been tight. Nigga how you gone rob my bitch for all her jewelry and give it to that Section 8 hoe! You betrayed me dawg. Go home, yo' bitch waiting for you!" He hung up.

I tried to call him back over and over again, but he didn't pick up. I flew out their house leaving the door wide open. Darryl was saying something behind me, but I wasn't paying him any mind. I sped all the way to Amanda's house, which was 18 blocks away. I got there, and saw that the door was wide open. I upped both of my .40 Glock and dashed inside and up the stairs. Her upstairs door was open a crack. I nudged it open more with my foot.

"Amanda, Amanda, baby I'm here. I'm here baby." The house was dark and quiet. I crept through the kitchen and into the living room. Still, I heard nothing. "Amanda, Amanda, baby. Where you at?"

I got to the hallway that led to her bedroom. The door was closed. I took a deep breath, twisted the knob and pushed the door in. What I saw made me fall to my knees. There, lying in the middle of the bed was Amanda spread eagle, naked, dead. Her stomach had been sliced down the middle, between her legs was our deceased unborn child. Amanda's neck was cut from ear to ear, on side of her leg lay her two sons, tied with gags in their mouths. I thought they were alive until I looked closer and saw the small holes on the backs of their heads, and blood.

My phone rang and I saw that it was Rallo's

number. "You sick mutha—"

"Nigga, you wanna war, lets war. See me before I see you!" He hung up.

I looked over Amanda again feeling the tears course down my face. I walked closer to the bed and picked up my unborn child, a little girl with the umbilical cord still attached. I kissed her on the forehead.

Chapter 13
Roman

It took me a whole week before I even got the chance to get close to Sazo`n. Champ gave me the low-down on a beach party that was going down that Friday. It was being thrown by some Haitans that him and Moeshe dealt with. The party was private, but I got an invitation. It was delivered by this chocolate dime. She knocked on my door at 6 in the morning on that Friday. When I opened the door, she handed me the invite. Before I could say anything to her she walked away and hopped in a droptop Maybach.

"Don't be late, the Zoes getting down!" She yelled with a mouth full of gold.

That night, I packed my whole hunter's kit. I knew damn well I wasn't gone get the chance to pop him in broad daylight, or at night around a bunch of people. I had visions of slicing his throat and getting back to Chicago by Saturday. I was homesick and missing my people.

When I got to the sectioned off portion of the beach, there was a line of security guards shaking people down for invitations. I handed them mine and avoided the pat search by slipping the big goofy a hundred-dollar bill. He slipped a bracelet around my right wrist that had a yacht on it. I eased into the party.

There was broads everywhere, wearing nothing but G-strings. I kept losing my focus. I got approached by so many broads of all different nationalities. I knew I was gone have to hit Miami up again on some party shit.

They had some rappers on the stage getting off! The dudes had the crowd hype. There was about 300 people around and everybody was having a good time. It looked like a small fair, overlooking the ocean. I avoided the sand as much as I could. I didn't want that shit in my sandals, so I walked all way around until I was directly in front of the stage, mixed in with the crowd while the fat black rapper from Miami rapped that he was the Boss! I nodded and scanned the crowed until I saw, Sazo`n.

He was directly in the middle of the pack, his arms around a Spanish girl and a light skinned black one. He had so much gold around his neck it was almost cheesy. I slowly made my way through the crowd until I was standing directly behind him. And the whole night, when he moved, I moved. He didn't even seem to notice me because he had so much pussy around him.

By the time I got my chance to get at him, I was so aggravated. I almost took a chance on killing him in the crowd. But then I heard him tell one of the girls that he'd be back, he had to take a piss. I looked toward the sky, and said thank you.

I followed him into the restrooms at a safe distance when I got to the door, two drunk studs came out talking loud and slurring. They bumped into me and I apologized. They just laughed and kept stepping

Sazo'n shook his head. "Some niggas ain't got no respect." He said walking into a stall.

I quickly looked around the bathroom, noting that there was only one Mexican dude left in there with us at the urinal. He had to be at least 40. He pressed his stomach in the porcelain grunting and groaning, struggling to get his urine to flow. I heard him cussing in Spanish. Finally, after trying for what seemed like forever to me, he gave up and hit the handle on the side, slurring curse words the whole time while washing his hands.

As soon as he left out, I locked the door, hoping that nobody would come trying to get in for at least two minutes. I knew that that was next to impossible, but I had to hope. I reached into the small of my back and slid up two Davucci Blades, both gleaming. I crouched down and peeked around the corner of the long row of stalls. I didn't see Sazo`n , so I looked under all the stalls until I located his Gucci's. Sure enough, he had his pants down taking a shit, his last one in life.

I walked casually down the stalls and slipped into the one right next to his. I closed the door real lightly and stepped on to the toilet seat, very cautiously. I peeked over the top into his stall. I had to balance my weight carefully because one of the hinges were loose, making the toilet seat shift sideways. Nevertheless, I knew I had to hurry because time was not on my side.

When I peeked over and down, I couldn't help but smile, then my heart started beating real fast. Sazo`n was seated on the toilet, with his pants down, a belt around his left arm, sliding a needle into his veins. When he pressed down on the syringe, the poison entered his veins from the heroin. He sighed and leaned his head back with his eyes closed, running his tongue across his dry lips. I saw that his neck was exposed, and his mouth was wide open.

I took the Davucci by the blade, cocked back and flung it down with all of my might. It connected landing right on his Adam's apple, I threw the other one, catching him to the left of the first one. He sprawled forward, so I jumped over the top of the stall landing on his back. His body folded in half with his knees pressed into his chest. I could hear him gurgling on his own blood.

I grabbed him by the hair after slipping another Davucci from my waist and slit his throat from one ear to the next. Securing my first two weapons, wiping his blood off on his shirt. I climbed back out of the stall, leaving him inside of the one he was in leaning back against the wall. I slid my weapons back into their holsters and unlocked the door, just as three young teens who looked like rappers inched past me.

It was pitch dark outside. I was glad for that. I easily slipped away from the party, locating my whip. Everything had gone smoothly, and I couldn't have asked for a better fate or so I thought.

Chapter 14
Scooby

I started to missing my daughter, so every day I found myself parked in front of her house hoping to catch a glimpse of her, which I almost always did. Her and my grandson both looked good and healthy. For that alone I was proud. I wanted so bad to talk to her. I wanted to hug my grandson, but I promised her mother a long time ago that I would never interfere with her or her brother's life. I walked out on them many, many years ago, before they were old enough to talk. It was a decision I regretted every living day of my life.

I drove away as a big truck pulled into her driveway and a sharply dressed old enemy stepped out of it. He glared at me and our eyes met. He tucked his coat back, showing me the handle of his gun. I continued on my way.

It took me another whole month to locate Rallo. I was at home with my old girlfriend Sharon, smoking rock after rock. Her eyes were so big it looked like they were about to pop out. I'm sure mine were just as bucked. But I kept reloading that pipe, and burning away my sorrows. My whole head was numb, my breath stank, and I'd had the same clothes on for two weeks, including underwear. My beard was full, and the hair sticking out my nose had boogers stuck to it, but I didn't care because I was getting high and floating far away from reality.

Sharon dug in her nose and popped the booger. I heard it smack the wall in front of her. She grabbed her beer and took a long swallow. "Scooby, I'm glad you take so good care of me." She began, while loading her pipe, flicking the lighter. "I swear anything you want I'm gone do to you tonight. I want some of that dope dick." She lit the rock and inhaled causing the end of her glass pipe to turn black.

Afterwards, she smacked her lips and scratched between her legs. She raised her hips off the couch and turned her butt sideways. Farting three times, the last one sound like four in one. "Whew, I don't know what I ate, but it show got my stomach in knots. I gotta quit messing with Rallo ass. Every time he cook, it mess up my stomach when I eat it." She lifted up and farted again, waving her hand through the air holding her nose.

I dropped my tools on the table. "Say what, Sharon? Where you see Rallo at?" My heartbeat sped up; due to the fact it was already racing from the dope. It was a wonder how I didn't kill over.

"Chile!" Him and that white girl stay right down on Bishop. He done smoked her out a house and home. That white woman gotta be about 80 pounds now, and he ain't but a 100. All they do is smoke and fight. Last time I was over there she had two black eyes, and he had one." She started cracking up kicking her legs in the air, exposing her scar-ridden thighs from hard living. Laughing so hard made her pass a series of farts which she acted like didn't happen.

I slid to the edge of my seat. "You know exactly where they stay, Sharon?" I could barely contain my excitement.

"Why?" She paused now looking me over closely.

I slid an ounce across the table the whole time looking in her eyes.

"Because I want you to take me to them."

Hood Rich

Chapter 15
Roman

I'd been back in Chicago two weeks, laying low. Binkey was in the ending stages of her trial and it seemed like she was set to beat the murders. Over the course of six months I'd been leaving those same machete's all around the south side of Chicago, and I'd killed three cats with the same brand, tossing the machetes away, but into a place I knew the police would find them. Besides the murder weapon, they had nothing on Binkey. They didn't even have circumstantial evidence, because she had no motive, and no record. Even the D.A was bored with the case and wanted to move on. I knew that I would be getting my Queen home soon.

Pulling up at Kelly's house was no easy task for me. Even though she had blessed me with a precious healthy baby girl, every time I saw her I felt betrayed. I hated snitches, and I hated what her snitching had done to my Queen. Yet, I picked my daughter up twice a week. Most times me and her never spoke. She'd have her ready and at the door when I came. She would hand her to me, and I'd leave. That was how things went this particular day. While she was handing me my daughter, I looked over her shoulder into the house and saw some dude sitting in the living room with his boxers on and no shirt. Now I didn't care what she did, or what she did it with, but due to the fact that we had a daughter, I felt the stud's attire was unacceptable, and I told her that.

She got defensive and asked me why I was worried about what was going on in her house, then slammed the door in my face. It took everything I had in me to not kick her door in, go in there, and change both they ass. But I simply kissed my daughter's forehead and left.

When we arrived at Rihanna's crib, Mya jumped down the steps of the porch and ran to my Navigator. She loved her little sister, Jewel. I slid Jewel into her arms, walked on to the porch and gave Rihanna a hug and friendly peck on the cheek. She smiled.

"I cooked up a plate. It's in the microwave if you want it."

"No pork?"

"No pork, Roman." She rolled her eyes.

I laughed, walked into the house. But something didn't feel right. It was like time slowed all the way down. I pushed start on the microwave, looked into the refrigerator and pulled out a two-liter bottle of Grape pop. I heard Rihanna yelling something to Mya, something about bring the baby in and then it happened. She let out a scream that damn near gave me a heart attack! Then, the house was rocking.

Blocka! Blocka! Blocka! Taat... Taat.... Taat.... Taat...Taat...Blocka! Blocka! Blocka! Boom! Boom! Boom! Boom! Taat....Taat... Taat... Boom! Boom!

The windows shattered, along with the plaster on the walls. I dropped to the floor, upped my 40 Glock, and low crawled toward the front door. I saw Rihanna running outside as the shooting continued to grow worst. The sofa was in shreds, pictures fell from the walls, the big screen TV fell forward and crashed into the table. I covered my head trying to get to the door. When I looked up, I saw my daughters Mya and Jewel get snatched into a Suburban, it sped sway. A

Spanish man glared as he yanked my daughter in by her hair. She almost dropped Jewel but held on to her.

Then Rihanna, I saw the first bullet hit Rihanna in the chest and then her stomach. She was literally stood up while three Mexican men pumped over a hundred bullets into her body. I started to shoot out the door catching one in his shoulder, he dropped his weapon I kept popping, while the other two loaded into a Benz, but not before they shot him in the dome. They sped away with six trucks following close behind.

Hood Rich

Chapter 16
Scooby

It was after 12 am, on a cold night in March. Everything was mapped out and I was ready to meet Rallo with the help of Sharon who was oblivious as to what was really going on. I hid on the side of the door while she knocked at their backdoor.

"Who is it?" I heard Rallo's familiar voice ask. I started to get giddy.

"Rallo, open this damn door, it's Sharon. I told you I was coming over to share with you and Julie since y'all shared with me on check day last Friday. I got a nice amount from my white trick." She added.

When the lock turned, I almost lost my breath. "Girl get yo' sexy ass in here and let's get our groove on!" He hollered.

Sharon stepped in, and when Rallo turned to close the door I swept out of the shadows and pushed him into the house and upped my .40 caliber, aiming it right at his head. He fell forward to the floor turning around looking at me with eyes so buck it was like he was seeing death, and he couldn't escape it. His face went from that pf panic, to an evil snarl.

"You know what main-man? If it's my time to go, then let me go. You got me, so fuck you nigga. You jive   turkey   son-of-a—"
Boom! Boom! Boom! I walked up on him and emptied the clip and reloaded. His body twisted, his face was mush, after all the shots.

Sharon stared, open mouthed. I saw the piss running down her thighs. I wasn't usually the type to hurt women, but there was no way I could let her live.

I saw Julie run across the living room toward the front door. I shot three times catching her in the back, she fell, unmoving. By this time Sharon had dropped to her knees praying, rocking back and forth. I knelt down in back of her and put her in a choke hold. "I'm sorry baby." with a quick twist, I snapped her neck and let her go. She fell on to her stomach, her head turned almost backwards! I checked on Julie; she had no pulse. The rest of the house was empty. I took the dope from Sharon and poured it on the floor and then fled.

Chapter 17
Heaven

Three months since my nieces had been missing and our family still hadn't heard anything. This was a direct attack to our bloodline, and it was driving our family crazy. I'd never seen Roman so distraught, and Kelly was still in the hospital under psychiatric evaluation. I was so worried about something happening to Tarig Junior that I took him out of school and we both move to St. Louis, Missouri. I wasn't taking no chances of something happening to my baby. His father was set to come home in six more months and I wanted us to both be intact.

I'd found a nice building to open a salon in, and at the end of the month I would be back in business. I felt good to be away from the drama. I felt like St. Louis would give us a new start. Pam had moved out here four months ago and she was doing well. There were so many opportunities here, so far so good. The people were welcoming. There was some racism, but, what could you do, that was life.

We were at a bodega because Pam wanted to buy some cigarettes. I came in with her because the city was still new to me and it kinda gave me an uneasy feeling, especially since there was so much going on inside my family. As we were at the counter getting ready to purchase our items, Pam joked that I was starting to look older, and I nudged her with my elbow.

"Girl whatever, I know I still look damn good." I said, batting my eyelashes and poking my hips out. "For your information I turn heads everywhere I go.

So, how you love that?" I threw five fingers up in her face and twisted my hand, rolling my eyes at the same time.

She sucked her teeth. "Yeah, that's cause they wondering how an old woman could be dressed up like a teenager. They probably thought you had on your daughter's clothes." She teased, placing her hand on her back and limping in front of me like an old woman.

I took a deep breath. "Okay, now you just hurting my feelings." I lowered my head and poked my lip out.

She laughed. "I'm sorry Grandma. Naw, I'm just playing, you know I love you. But damn girl, don't tell me you getting soft. We still Chicago-bred." She closed her eyes and hit her chest. "Chi-town!"

I started cutting up. She had me rolling, holding my stomach. "Never soft baby, I'm still Windy City, don't lose yourself." I said, trying to act hard.

Pam nodded, "That's right, that's what I'm talking about." She went in her pocket and pulled out a dew bills, counting them. "Girl throw that little pop and chips on the counter, I got you. After all them times you done bought me stuff." She grabbed them out my hand.

I rolled my eyes. "Yeah, most of them you returned, that's why I don't give your ass receipts with the gifts no more. Shid, I'm hip to that. "I looked her up and down and shook my head. "Umm huh."

"Girl you tripping, I—" Pam began.

Just then, two teenagers came into the store. The first one was a big boy. He had to be about 260 pounds, and every bit of 6 feet 5 inches tall. He had a white t-shirt on and black baggy pants. He looked like Biggie Smalls, His friend was slim, also dressed like a hip-hop rapper. He had plenty jewelry around his neck, his black pants sagged, under his white t-shirt. His fitted, St. Louis Cardinals turned to the back.

The big one came and bumped Pam out the way. She almost fell down. "Excuse you!" She glared, holding on to the rack behind her.

He didn't pay her any attention. He reached across the counter and snatched a box of cigarettes. The Asian man tried to grab it away from him, but he palmed the clerk's head and flung him back toward the liquor behind him. "Put it on my tab, ma`fucka!" He snarled.

His skinny friend grabbed an Apple juice and big bag of popcorn, laughing the whole time. "Uh, excuse us ladies, we mean no disrespect toward you black Queens." He smiled, and they left.

The Asian man was already on the phone with the police, waving his arms frantically, wiping the sweat from his forehead. He held up one finger to us, while he finished describing the two young men who had to be well on their way by now. I felt bad, the Asian man looked as if he wanted to cry.

"Damn these kids today ain't got no respect. Now, this man just trying to run a business. They make us all look bad." Pam shook her head.

"Girl, I pray for lord Jesus, I would break Tarig Junior's neck if he ever thought about doing some mess like that. Umm, his ass would be out!" I closed my eyes, just picturing it.

"My future husband would never do something

like that, so get it together." She said, snapping fingers in my face.

"Move!" I swatted her hand away. "And you got to be crazy if you think your grown ass gone corrupt my baby! Shid! You betta go rob somebody else's cradle. Talking `bout future husband. Please!"

"Whatever, that's me right there. He gon` be fine too. Our babies gone be prettier than Kim and Kanye's." Now her eyes was closed, with her arms wrapped around herself.

I pulled her arm, jerking her out her zone. "Babies! Aww, now you really tripping, by the time my son ready to have kids all your stuff gone be dried up. Let's not forget, you older than me." I said, poking her on the shoulder.

"Stooppp!" She swatted my finger away.

"I can help you now." The clerk said.

Pam stepped up to the counter. "Look, I wanna pay for them cigars they took too, along with the pop and potato chips, popcorn, whatever. I apologize for their behavior." She smiled putting our things on the counter.

He nodded, a tear threatening to roll down his cheek. "Thank you so much miss." He took the twenty-dollar bill from her and rang up the items.

The St. Louis sun baked us as soon as we stepped out of the air-conditioned store. Not only was it hot, but the humidity made it sticky and nearly unbearable. I felt like I couldn't breathe. My Michael Kors pants were way too tight, so was my halter. Damn, I could have gone without the bra I had on. I looked over at Pam and she looked just as miserable. She had her tongue stuck out like she was ready to pass out in any moment.

"Can you explain to me why we chose to walk all the way to this store?" I asked. There were people everywhere, throwing water on each other.

"Girl, cause, we needed a walk instead of driving every damn where. Take in the scenery. Enjoy St. Louis, this is a beautiful place to be." She said waving her hand through the air and pointing at random sites and people. I knew that she had spent 7 years of her life in St. Louis when she moved from Chicago with her mother and stepfather. When she came back at age 8, we met and became best friends.

"Scenery? Girl I done seen ghetto folks before throwing water on each other. Sistas walking around with head scarfs on half naked, pushing strollers. I done seen lil boys playing catch football in the middle of the street before. And them dudes over there ganged up passing blunts and bottles back and forth while they harass the hood chicks, is all a regular occurrence to me. Girl all is reminiscent of the Chi."

Pam, looked around. "Damn I guess you right." She shrugged her shoulders as we turned down a quiet block. "Let me get a sip of that pop."

I handed it to her. We were in the middle of the block when those same two teenagers came out of a gangway and started walking toward us. I froze in my tracks, grabbing Pam's wrist. She looked up and saw them too.

"Aww shit!" Her face grew worried.

Then I started panicking, "What should we do?" Just then a police car bent the corner hard and slammed on its breaks.

The officer started yelling something at the boys. They turned looking at him, then turned to keep walking away. He yelled again, and the big teen threw down his bottled water and ran over to the driver's side window of the police car shouting inside at the officer. We couldn't hear what he was yelling, but he looked angry. After he said his peace, he started to walk off again. Then the driver's door opened, he snarled something at the young men, and this infuriated the bigger teen. He turned around and charged at the white officer, the cops ran back into his car. The big teen reached inside and we both jumped when we heard the gun shot, then another. The big teen backed up with his hands in the air begging the officer to stop. His friend ran away leaving him to fend for his self.

The officer stepped out the car with his gun pointed at the teen. The young man held his hands up higher. We were able to see blood pouring down his wrist. What happened next made me wrap my arms around Pam.

The officer looked both ways, frowned his face and fired his weapon over and over again, shooting the young man dead into the street. He stood over him with an evil look on his face, then radioed to his dispatcher. By this time, me and Pam were running full speed into the other direction. I felt sick and I was determined to get the hell out of Missouri.

Chapter 18
Roman

I was as lost as I had ever been. Four months and still no word on my princesses. I took to drinking heavily and smoking blunt after blunt. Who am I kidding, I was tooting powder now too? I was trying to escape the pain that had enveloped me. I knew deep down that my kids' kidnapping had to do with my actions. My past had caught up with me, I just didn't know which enemy had struck. All I remembered was a bunch of Spanish assassins. I had at least 9 Spanish bodies under my belt, not including that move in Texas. Truth be told I didn't know where to strike or who to strike. I was missing Mya like crazy and Jewel was also in my every dream and nightmare. Kelly was in a psychiatric hospital, and Binkey had beat the murders, but still got sent to North for some battery she'd committed. She beat some girl senseless; they gave her three years, she'd be home in one, and I couldn't wait. My son Jaheim was with my grandmother Gwen. She was holding him down and making sure he was good. She had recently moved to Madison to be closer to Seven and Brittany, who were doing damn good in school.

Seven was killing on that basketball court and was deciding on whether or not to enter the Draft. Brittany was going for her master's and was two years away from getting it.

My relationship with Champ was still strong, even though for a minute it got rocky after him and Heaven split. He took it on the chin though, and between us business pressed forward. After my daughter's got snatched I pulled 6 hits for him. In front of me now was over 750 thousand dollars of blood money. I had two kilos of cocaine on the floor, an Ak-47 on my lap and a straw in one hand tooting to ease the pain.

Wednesday night was hot and humid with the rain pelting on top of the trucks making it sound almost like hail, I laid back in my Pop's Escalade. We were parked in front of his Mansion, in the driveway. In the background was the O' Jays, "For The Love of Money." Pops leaned his seat back and nodded.

"So, what's good Pop? Why you call me out here tonight?" I pulled on the blunt and inhaled deeply. The smoke scorched my chest, but it felt good just the same. The seat was heated and vibrated softly under my ass. I was relaxed. His dashboard had a 9" screen playing The Mack as I passed Pops the blunt.

"I got one more move I want you to take care of for me son, and this is personal." He pulled on the blunt and kept talking with smoke coming through his teeth. "I want you to torture this muthafucka too! Do him really good, because he betrayed your father." He leaned forward and dumped the ashes in the ashtray.

I took the blunt back from him. "No problem, just tell me who and where, and I'll let you know when it's done. I hit the blunt three times hard and inhaled, passing it back to him with my jaws puffed up like I had a mouthful of food.

He took it back. "Nawl son for this, I wanna be present."

* * *

"Heyyyy baby! As-salam-Alaikum! Binkey said

sliding into my arms.

I leaned down and our lips connected, tongues wrestling. I heard her breathing hard. I rolled my head down and bit her on the neck and sucked. She reached between us and grabbed my dick. Then our lips connected again. I squeezed her titties.

"Hey!"

We both snapped apart and looked at the C.O behind the desk. He started to wag his finger as if saying, that's a no-no. I nodded and kissed my boo one more time, before we sat down with our fingers interlocked.

"Damn ma', walaikum As Salam. Umm!" I looked her over and with no make up my baby was still gorgeous. Her dreads were getting long, and her face a lil fatter, but it made her look gorgeous. She kept kissing my hand and saying how much she missed me.

After we did our lovey-dovies, her face took on a serious expression.

"Baby, what's going on, I know you better than anybody else, talk to me." She squeezed my hand and moved closer, looking around the small prison visiting room.

"I gotta make one last move and I'm done boo!" I looked her straight in the eyes now, squeezing her hand back to emphasize my point.

"But you said you were through, Roman. Why? Who is it?" Her eyes were starting to glaze up.

"Somebody for my old man." This time I avoided her eyes. I scanned the visiting room making eye contact with a Red-Bone sista who licked her lips at me.

"Why he need you to do it! He got all that fucking money. He can have anybody take care of that business, yet he want to keep putting you under the gun. I don't understand that shit!" She frowned.

"We got a family to think about. Don't he know that, and if he do, he sho' don't act like he do. That man gon' get you seriously hurt one day. Damn baby, do you have too?" She sounded concerned, lightly touching my cheek.

"Boo, after this, I'ma chill. You got my word on that." We sat silent for a long time.

"I just don't feel right. My gut telling me something ain't right baby. Can you please not do this one. Tell him to get somebody else." Her voice started to break up. Tears flowed down her cheeks.

"Last one boo, I promise."

Chapter 19
Scooby

I sat in front of my big screen watching Scarface in white boxers and a black silk robe. Well, I couldn't really say I was watching the movie. It was more or so watching me. I was nodding in and out, scratching occasionally. After all the bullshit I'd been through, I'd graduated from smoking rock, to shooting heroin, and I was feeling damn good.

I wrapped my belt around my left arm and tied it tight, pulling it with my teeth. Once it was fastened, I smacked my veins until they popped up, poked the needle in the thick noodle of a vein and pressed down on the syringe. When the poison hit my blood stream; all my cares went away. I was on cloud 9, and nothing else mattered.

I licked my lips and blew my nose into a Kleenex from the table. Tony Montana was on the screen chopping shit up with an Ak. The movie was almost over, but I would only start it from the beginning again and again.

My life had gone downhill fast. I felt like a loser. What had I become in nearly 50 years of living? Nothing! Not a damn thing. My plan was to do as much dope as I could until it took the breath out of my body. The next life had to be better than this one. For some reason, I started missing my first love. I got to imagining how things were back in high school. Sexy Deborah is what they called her. 5 foot 5, red skin and brown eyes. She was bad! Country fed and country bred. We were inseparable. She gave me two kids and I gave her walking papers and a reason to hate men for eternity.

Everybody I came into contact with, I wound up hurting. It was like I was cursed. I put the heroin on the spoon and put the flame underneath it until it became liquid, drew it up with my syringe, smacked my arm, and stabbed into the same vein feeling an instant orgasm.

I slid a Newport out the pack and lit it. With the remote, I activated my sound system. Ronald Isley's voice serenaded through the room. "I-I-I keep hearing footsteps baby.... In the darkkkk... I-I-I-I-I." I tapped my fingers on the arm of the couch to the beat, shaking my head back and forth. "Ooh Weee! Them boys bad. Ain't a band alive, that can—"

Paid in Blood 2

Chapter 20
Armani

"Fuck with them, is that what you were going to say?" I stepped out of the shadows with an automatic shot gun pointed directly at him. "Surprise!"

Roman, whipped a wire around his neck and pulled him up until he was standing with my son behind him choking the addict to death.

"That's enough son, sit him in that chair right there and tie him up."

It took Roman less than two minutes to secure him. He came and stood beside me. We watched Scooby squirm, trying to shake his self free with a gag stuffed deeply in his mouth. He looked pitiful. Look at the man he'd become, filth.

I handed the shotgun to my son Roman, tightened the gloves on my hand, cocked back and swung, punching him square in the nose with a right, and in the eye with my left. He was split open good.

"You just couldn't stay away could you, you had to break the rules!" I growled before swinging and splitting him open further. He still had a belt wrapped around his arm, probably from his heroin use.

" Mmmph! Mmmph! Mmmm! Mmmmph!"

"What's that? I can't hear you muthafucka. Sound like you got something in your mouth!" I swung, busting his lip, then back handed him so hard he spit the gag out.

"You punk bitch, fuck you! That's my daughter, I can see her whenever I want too. That's my baby girl! You—"

I punched him over and over. "You left them you

145

son-of-a-bitch. She's my child. You were supposed to stay away! You... dope...fiend...sick... son... of... a... bitch!" His head rattled back and forth on his neck. His face was so bruised it swelled up like a pumpkin, but still he smiled. He turned his head to the side and spit a glob of blood against the wall. He started laughing.

"Ahhh! Kill me, muthafucka! Kill me, but the truth will always be the truth. Heaven is my daughter! That's my baby girl. No matter what you do to me, nothing will change that." He spit again and one of his teeth ricocheted off the wall and hit the floor.

"Pops, what he talking about?" Roman began, standing in front of Scooby with a look of confusion.

I waved him off. "Nothing son, this muthafucka is delirious." I reached back to swing again but Roman stood in my way. "Boy move." I began.

"I wanna know what he talking about." He glared at me.

Scooby smiled, "Yeah, tell him how I'm his father too. Tell him how Deborah was my first love. Tell him why his daughter's been snatched muthafucka. My granddaughters. Tell him why Rihanna is dead. Tell him how your doctor friend killed his mother. Tell him the truth. Tell him how you cashed in on his mother and her businesses." He hissed.

Roman perked up. "What he talking about, Pop?" He snarled sticking his hand under his shirt.

I stuttered, "Son, he just, I mean that shit he saying is just. Well, first of all I don't know this muthafucka."

"Naw hold on! He know my momma name, my

sister name, and he knew about my daughters. Something, ain't right. Now tell me what's going on?"

Hood Rich

Chapter 21
Roman

I saw that nervous look appear across my Pops face and something in me knew that this dope fiend wasn't lying. Right before me I saw my whole world flip. Everything that I had ever known was a lie. I couldn't control my thoughts and before I knew what was happening I had a .44 Desert Eagle pressed to my old man's forehead, and he had the shotgun pressed to my chest. "Pop, please tell me this stud lying man, please."

I saw tears sail down my old man's cheeks, and I knew he had basically told me everything I needed to know. "I'm sorry son, I don't know what to say. I—"

Boom! Somebody had kicked in the door. I turned to look, and my old man fell to his knees and shot me right through the thigh. The bullet tripped me, and I fell on my face.

When I looked up, he was running out the back door turning around once to shoot three shots at the thugs that kicked the door. Then, he was gone. They shot at him six times, I didn't know if he was hit.

"Lay it down niggas! Lay it down!"

I laid on my stomach, as they ransacked the house and robbed me and Scooby. Then they tied us up and left. I was in so much pain from the blast that I passed out. When I came to, my grandmother was staring down at me with a worried expression on her face. I tried to move but felt weak. There were IV's in my left hand, when I tried to move my wrist it was restricted by a u and so was the left. I was confused and hella dazed. "Grandma, what's going on?"

She patted my chest. "That lying, dirty dope addict is your father, unfortunately baby. You and Heaven have the same father, and so does Brittany and Seven. They are Calvin's children, Armani, your Pops, or whatever you want to call him now."

She shook her head. "I told that girl a long time ago that neither one of them men was no good. Now Calvin got all them damn restaurants, and done got your daughters kidnapped messing with them damn Cartels across the border. They say he double crossed somebody, and now our family under the gun. That no good trifling man done ran off somewhere leaving us to fight his battles. Umm." She shook her head, her curly gray hair swinging back and forth.

"Baby one thing you gotta know, is that your momma, ain't never been no damn tool. She knew Calvin was up to no good, so she left a whole lot of money to me to put up and that's just what I did." She pulled me by the collar. "You listen here, you gone build up your army and you gone go avenge your momma, and find your daughters. I done called 12 of your closest cousins from Haiti and they flying in tomorrow. It's time to go to war and it's time to show that Cartel what real Assassins are all about. Now you look at me here. You got my blood in you. That in your veins is from me! You do everything that you have too to find Calvin and bring his ass to me. I owe your mother a favor. That was my only daughter!" She took her glasses off. "You kill with everything that you got!" she hissed. "Do I make myself clear."

I nodded. "Yes ma'am." She uncuffed me and slid the iron into her purse. I looked at her bewildered and for the first time noticed blood on her white blouse.

She held her finger up. "Ssssssshhhhhh!" She pointed downward.

I peeked and saw the guard under my bed, with blood dripping from a deep gash in his throat. His eyes were wide open.

"Come on and get out that bed. We gotta get you to a safe house. Come on!"

Hood Rich

Chapter 22
Heaven

I couldn't stand still; I was too anxious. *Oh my God can he hurry up*. My nerves were getting the best of me. Tarig Junior was pacing back and forth as well. He had to be as nervous as I was. And then I saw him coming through the gates with a duffel bag. Tears welled up in my eyes, and my heart turned over. Me and Tarig Junior raced to meet him.

He picked me up first, turning me around in a circle, loading me up with kisses. Then he picked up his son and repeated the process. I was so happy that I wrapped my arms around the both of them. I'd finally had my family. After so many years of waiting, and fighting, my baby was out of that prison.

"Damn, baby, it feel so good to be free. Let's get out of here right now." He pulled me by the hand.

We were no more than six feet away from my car in the parking lot, when 6 black hummers appeared all at once, surrounding it. My heart dropped. I started thinking about the war against my family and the many enemies we had. My first instinct was to wrap my arms around Tarig Junior. His father stood in front of us protectively.

The doors to the trucks opened up and at least 20 Deadhead's got out in all black fatigues with Army boots on. They looked menacing and heartless. Their eyes were soul-less. They reeked of death. I just knew that our lives were over, but then the crowd of parted and from within them appeared Roman, with a slight limp. He extended a hand to Tarig, then hugged him.

"Brother, welcome back to freedom but however your services are needed right now. Our family is at war, and if we don't meet this head on. They gone be the next victims." He pointed to me and my son.

I saw Tarig frown up, then he started to nod. "Give me three days with my family, then come get me." He hit his chest.

Roman nodded, they bumped fists, and my brother walked off. "I love y'all and be safe." He ordered a Hummer of terrorists to follow us home.

I looked over to Tarig and tears began flowing as we loaded into our Caravan. I was going to lose him already. My baby was joining our family's war, and there was no telling what the outcome would be. I had three days to enjoy him, and I would make them count. I had too.

Chapter 23
Seven

"Damn, it feel like it's hot as hell in here don't it?" I stuck my finger inside my shirt collar and pulled, trying to get some air to flow inside. My throat was dry, my palms sweaty, and I felt like my vision was getting blurry. Everything that was taking place with my family was starting to get the better of me. It had gotten so bad that I couldn't even visit Chicago, I hadn't seen Roman or Brittany in nearly a year, and there was no telling when I would be able to see them again. Roman, from what the streets said, was in full Taliban mode. He was causing so much ruckus that cats were putting him in their rap lyrics. I had never been more worried about my brother than I was as of late. I fanned my face with the program in my hand.

The huge arena was packed with cameras and journalists. There were flashes going on and off. Soft murmuring, and even a baby crying. I felt like I was in a sardine can.

"Boy be still, you just nervous." Brittany whispered. She was easy breezy, like she didn't have a care in the world.

"Baby just chill, huh, give me that program." Kendra grabbed it from me and started fanning my face. It was just like her to always know what to do. Over the last few years, we'd grown so close. I knew that I was going to marry her, I just didn't know when.

"Shahs, alright, here they go." Brittany said looking at the sharply dressed man as he took the stage.

The audience grew quiet, cameras could be heard flickering. The white man adjusted his suit and stepped up to the microphone. He cleared his throat. "And with the second overall pick in the N.B.A draft, The Chicago Bulls, select,." He paused to open the envelope. "Mr. Seven James."

I felt my heart stop. Brittany shot up and wrap her arms around me, following by Kendra and my grandmother. They were clapping and hugging each other. Time for me seemed to go in slow motion. It felt like I took a year to make it up on stage, where I shook hands with the commissioner, and then the team's owner.

"Welcome to the NBA, we are so grateful to have you, we have some big things in store." I was breathless.

To Be Continued. . .
Paid in Blood 3
Coming Soon

Submission Guideline

Submit the first three chapters of your completed manuscript to ldpsubmissions@gmail.com, subject line: Your book's title. The manuscript must be in a .doc file and sent as an attachment. Document should be in Times New Roman, double spaced and in size 12 font. Also, provide your synopsis and full contact information. If sending multiple submissions, they must each be in a separate email.

Have a story but no way to send it electronically? You can still submit to LDP/Ca$h Presents. Send in the first three chapters, written or typed, of your completed manuscript to:

LDP: Submissions Dept
Po Box 870494
Mesquite, Tx 75187

DO NOT send original manuscript. Must be a duplicate.

Provide your synopsis and a cover letter containing your full contact information.

Thanks for considering LDP and Ca$h Presents.

Hood Rich

BOW DOWN TO MY GANGSTA

By **Ca$h**

TORN BETWEEN TWO

By **Coffee**

BLOOD STAINS OF A SHOTTA **III**

By **Jamaica**

STEADY MOBBIN **III**

By **Marcellus Allen**

RENEGADE BOYS IV

By Meesha

BLOOD OF A BOSS **VI**

SHADOWS OF THE GAME II

By **Askari**

LOYAL TO THE GAME **IV**

LIFE OF SIN **III**

By **T.J. & Jelissa**

A DOPEBOY'S PRAYER **II**

By **Eddie "Wolf" Lee**

IF LOVING YOU IS WRONG… **III**

By **Jelissa**

TRUE SAVAGE **VII**

By **Chris Green**

BLAST FOR ME **III**

DUFFLE BAG CARTEL **IV**

HEARTLESS GOON **II**

Paid in Blood 2

By **Ghost**

A HUSTLER'S DECEIT III

KILL ZONE **II**

BAE BELONGS TO ME III

SOUL OF A MONSTER III

By **Aryanna**

THE COST OF LOYALTY **III**

By **Kweli**

A GANGSTER'S SYN III

THE SAVAGE LIFE II

By **J-Blunt**

KING OF NEW YORK V

RISE TO POWER III

COKE KINGS IV

BORN HEARTLESS II

By **T.J. Edwards**

GORILLAZ IN THE BAY IV

De'Kari

THE STREETS ARE CALLING II

Duquie Wilson

KINGPIN KILLAZ IV

STREET KINGS III

PAID IN BLOOD III

Hood Rich

SINS OF A HUSTLA II

ASAD

TRIGGADALE III

Elijah R. Freeman

KINGZ OF THE GAME IV

Playa Ray

SLAUGHTER GANG IV

RUTHLESS HEART

By Willie Slaughter

THE HEART OF A SAVAGE II

By Jibril Williams

FUK SHYT II

By Blakk Diamond

THE DOPEMAN'S BODYGAURD II

By Tranay Adams

TRAP GOD II

By Troublesome

YAYO II

By S. Allen

GHOST MOB

Stilloan Robinson

KINGPIN DREAMS

By Paper Boi Rari

CREAM

By Yolanda Moore

<u>**Available Now**</u>

RESTRAINING ORDER **I & II**

By **CA$H & Coffee**

LOVE KNOWS NO BOUNDARIES **I II & III**

By **Coffee**

RAISED AS A GOON I, II, III & IV

BRED BY THE SLUMS I, II, III

BLAST FOR ME I & II

ROTTEN TO THE CORE I II III

A BRONX TALE I, II, III

DUFFEL BAG CARTEL I II III

HEARTLESS GOON

A SAVAGE DOPEBOY

HEARTLESS GOON

By **Ghost**

LAY IT DOWN **I & II**

LAST OF A DYING BREED

BLOOD STAINS OF A SHOTTA I & II

By **Jamaica**

LOYAL TO THE GAME

LOYAL TO THE GAME II

LOYAL TO THE GAME III

LIFE OF SIN I, II

By **TJ & Jelissa**

BLOODY COMMAS I & II

SKI MASK CARTEL I II & III

KING OF NEW YORK I II,III IV

RISE TO POWER I II

Hood Rich

COKE KINGS I II III

BORN HEARTLESS

By **T.J. Edwards**

IF LOVING HIM IS WRONG…I & II

LOVE ME EVEN WHEN IT HURTS I II III

By **Jelissa**

WHEN THE STREETS CLAP BACK I & II III

By **Jibril Williams**

A DISTINGUISHED THUG STOLE MY HEART I II & III

LOVE SHOULDN'T HURT I II III IV

RENEGADE BOYS I II III

By **Meesha**

A GANGSTER'S CODE I &, II III

A GANGSTER'S SYN I II

THE SAVAGE LIFE

By **J-Blunt**

PUSH IT TO THE LIMIT

By **Bre' Hayes**

BLOOD OF A BOSS **I, II, III, IV, V**

SHADOWS OF THE GAME

By **Askari**

THE STREETS BLEED MURDER **I, II & III**

THE HEART OF A GANGSTA I II& III

By **Jerry Jackson**

CUM FOR ME

CUM FOR ME 2

CUM FOR ME 3

CUM FOR ME 4

CUM FOR ME 5

An **LDP Erotica Collaboration**

BRIDE OF A HUSTLA **I II & II**

THE FETTI GIRLS **I, II& III**

CORRUPTED BY A GANGSTA I, II III, IV

BLINDED BY HIS LOVE

By **Destiny Skai**

WHEN A GOOD GIRL GOES BAD

By **Adrienne**

THE COST OF LOYALTY I II

By Kweli

A GANGSTER'S REVENGE **I II III & IV**

THE BOSS MAN'S DAUGHTERS

THE BOSS MAN'S DAUGHTERS II

THE BOSSMAN'S DAUGHTERS III

THE BOSSMAN'S DAUGHTERS IV

THE BOSS MAN'S DAUGHTERS **V**

A SAVAGE LOVE **I & II**

BAE BELONGS TO ME I II

A HUSTLER'S DECEIT I, II, III

WHAT BAD BITCHES DO I, II, III

SOUL OF A MONSTER I II

KILL ZONE

By **Aryanna**

A KINGPIN'S AMBITON

A KINGPIN'S AMBITION **II**

I MURDER FOR THE DOUGH

By **Ambitious**

TRUE SAVAGE

TRUE SAVAGE II

TRUE SAVAGE **III**

TRUE SAVAGE **IV**

TRUE SAVAGE **V**

TRUE SAVAGE **VI**

By **Chris Green**

A DOPEBOY'S PRAYER

By **Eddie "Wolf" Lee**

THE KING CARTEL **I, II & III**

By **Frank Gresham**

THESE NIGGAS AIN'T LOYAL **I, II & III**

By **Nikki Tee**

GANGSTA SHYT **I II &III**

By **CATO**

THE ULTIMATE BETRAYAL

By **Phoenix**

BOSS'N UP **I , II & III**

By **Royal Nicole**

I LOVE YOU TO DEATH

By Destiny J

I RIDE FOR MY HITTA

I STILL RIDE FOR MY HITTA

By **Misty Holt**

LOVE & CHASIN' PAPER

Paid in Blood 2

By **Qay Crockett**

TO DIE IN VAIN

SINS OF A HUSTLA

By **ASAD**

BROOKLYN HUSTLAZ

By **Boogsy Morina**

BROOKLYN ON LOCK I & II

By **Sonovia**

GANGSTA CITY

By **Teddy Duke**

A DRUG KING AND HIS DIAMOND I & II III

A DOPEMAN'S RICHES

HER MAN, MINE'S TOO I, II

CASH MONEY HO'S

By Nicole Goosby

TRAPHOUSE KING **I II & III**

KINGPIN KILLAZ I II III

STREET KINGS I II

PAID IN BLOOD **I II**

By **Hood Rich**

LIPSTICK KILLAH **I, II, III**

CRIME OF PASSION I & II

By **Mimi**

STEADY MOBBN' **I, II, III**

By **Marcellus Allen**

WHO SHOT YA **I, II, III**

Renta

Hood Rich

GORILLAZ IN THE BAY **I II III**

DE'KARI

TRIGGADALE I II

Elijah R. Freeman

GOD BLESS THE TRAPPERS I, II, III

THESE SCANDALOUS STREETS I, II, III

FEAR MY GANGSTA I, II, III

THESE STREETS DON'T LOVE NOBODY I, II

BURY ME A G I, II, III, IV, V

A GANGSTA'S EMPIRE I, II, III, IV

THE DOPEMAN'S BODYGAURD

Tranay Adams

THE STREETS ARE CALLING

Duquie Wilson

MARRIED TO A BOSS… I II III

By Destiny Skai & Chris Green

KINGZ OF THE GAME I II III

Playa Ray

SLAUGHTER GANG I II III

By Willie Slaughter

THE HEART OF A SAVAGE

By Jibril Williams

FUK SHYT

By Blakk Diamond

DON'T F#CK WITH MY HEART I II

By Linnea

ADDICTED TO THE DRAMA I II III

Paid in Blood 2

By Jamila

<u>YAYO</u>

By S. Allen

<u>TRAP GOD</u>

By Troublesome

Hood Rich

<u>BOOKS BY LDP'S CEO, CA\$H</u>

<u>TRUST IN NO MAN</u>

<u>TRUST IN NO MAN 2</u>

<u>TRUST IN NO MAN 3</u>

<u>BONDED BY BLOOD</u>

<u>SHORTY GOT A THUG</u>

<u>THUGS CRY</u>

<u>THUGS CRY 2</u>

<u>THUGS CRY 3</u>

<u>TRUST NO BITCH</u>

<u>TRUST NO BITCH 2</u>

<u>TRUST NO BITCH 3</u>

<u>TIL MY CASKET DROPS</u>

<u>RESTRAINING ORDER</u>

<u>RESTRAINING ORDER 2</u>

<u>IN LOVE WITH A CONVICT</u>

<u>Coming Soon</u>

BONDED BY BLOOD 2

BOW DOWN TO MY GANGSTA

Paid in Blood 2